Alesha Dixon first found fame as part of
BRIT-nominated and MOBO Award-winning
group Mis-Teeq, which achieved 2 platinum albums
and 7 top ten hits, before going on to become
a platinum-selling solo artist in her own right.
Alesha's appearance on *Strictly Come Dancing*
in 2007 led to her winning the series and
becoming a judge for three seasons.

Since then she has presented and hosted many TV
shows including CBBC dance show *Alesha's Street
Dance Stars, Children In Need, Comic Relief*, BBC1's *The
Greatest Dancer, America's Got Talent: The Champions,
Australia's Got Talent* and for a decade has been a hugely
popular judge on *Britain's Got Talent*.

# Also available

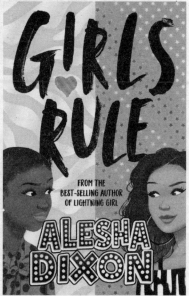

# LUNA WOLF
# ANIMAL WIZARD

## BY
## ALESHA DIXON

IN COLLABORATION WITH
### KATY BIRCHALL

ILLUSTRATED BY DEISE LINO

SCHOLASTIC

Published in the UK by Scholastic, 2023
1 London Bridge, London, SE1 9BG
Scholastic Ireland, 89E Lagan Road, Dublin Industrial Estate,
Glasnevin, Dublin, D11 HP5F

Text © Alesha Dixon, 2023
Illustrations by Deise Lino © Scholastic, 2023

The right of Alesha Dixon to be identified
as the author of this work has been asserted by her
under the Copyright, Designs and Patents Act 1988.

ISBN 978 0702 32410 9

Printed by CPI Group (UK) Ltd, Croydon, CR0 4YY
Papers used by Scholastic Children's Books are made
from wood grown in sustainable forests.

1 3 5 7 9 10 8 6 4 2

www.scholastic.co.uk

*For Kimmy, Shep, Roxy, Tyler, Teggy, Bobby,*
*Lola, Rosy, Daisy, Prince & Paris*

*Thank you for rescuing me... you rock!*

*X*

# PROLOGUE

## *Seven Years Ago: The Escape*

The door to the laboratory creaks open.

A woman tentatively steps in, treading as lightly as possible, slowly closing the door behind her. Her heart is thudding hard against her chest. She hardly dares to breathe.

In the dead of night there is no one in the laboratory but her. It's silent, except for a flutter of movement that comes from a series of large cages erected in the middle of the room. Atop one of the workstations that are spread out across the floor is a glass case. In the centre of it sits a jagged, gleaming

1

blue rock the size of a tennis ball.

Stopping by the door for a moment to gather her courage, the woman glances up at the security cameras fixed in the top corners of the ceiling. Their red lights blink back at her. Using her hand to smooth a crinkle in the arm of her lab coat, she lifts her chin up and confidently strides across the room.

She has to act as though everything is normal. The security guards didn't seem to think anything was amiss when she showed up for work just now, despite the time of night – after all, she's heading up this project and everyone knows that, on occasion, she's had to work early mornings and late nights. It didn't cross the guards' minds that she might be here for any other reason.

They won't know until the last minute that she's here to derail it all, and by then it will hopefully be too late to stop her. Now that she knows the truth about what's really been going on, about the *lies* that she's been fed, she won't let this project continue.

She stops at the glass box and, taking a deep breath,

places her hand on the security pad in front of it. It beeps in greeting before her fingerprints are scanned by red lasers. The light turns green as "ACCESS GRANTED" flashes across the screen. The glass shield lowers, leaving the blue rock on display.

She takes it in her hands, carrying it over to the cages where, producing a key from her pocket, she starts unlocking the large padlocks securing them.

One by one, the five cage doors swing open.

She hears the sound she's been waiting for looming in the distance: the whirring blades of a helicopter. It's time.

She quickly ushers the creatures out of the cages, and they follow her without question. With the blue rock tucked under her arm, she leads them to the large double doors on the opposite side of the room. As she hurries down the corridor with the escapees hot on her heels, she can hear the helicopter lowering through the air and coming in to land right outside.

Suddenly, alarms start blaring and red lights flash threateningly throughout the building. The guards have worked out that something is wrong. She doesn't have much time.

"Quickly!" she cries to the creatures following her, sprinting down the corridor to a fire exit.

She pushes it open, bursting out into the cold night air. The helicopter is waiting for them, its door sliding open. She hears the cries from the security guards somewhere behind her, and she knows it's only a matter of moments before they appear. Reaching the helicopter, she stops at the door to help her companions get in before her. Once they're all safely inside, she jumps in and instructs the pilot to "GO".

The door slides shut and the helicopter lifts from the ground.

Adrenaline pumping through her veins, she looks out of the window to the ground below where two security guards have come running and are now looking up at the helicopter helplessly as it rises higher and higher into the night sky.

A blonde curly-haired man with a thick moustache appears alongside them, wearing a white lab coat that matches hers. She didn't know he was here tonight; he must have been working late on something he'd been told to keep hidden from his colleagues.

*So many secrets.*

She was right not to trust him. She'd had that gut feeling about him from the start.

He shields his face with his arm and tries to keep steady on his feet against the wind force of the helicopter taking off. There's nothing he can do but watch her escape, the helicopter disappearing into the night. Running his hands through his hair, he roars in fury.

She doesn't breathe a sigh of relief until he's nothing but a tiny dot left behind.

*She did it.*

A few hours later, Dr Callahan steps nervously into the vast laboratory, hit by a wave of nausea as he sees a tall, suited, intimidating figure standing in the middle looking upon a row of huge, empty cages, their doors hanging open.

For the last year, Callahan has walked into this laboratory every morning with a feeling of great ambition and excitement for what they are creating here.

But today all he feels is fear and dread.

As the door clanks shut behind him, the suited man starts, irritated at being disturbed. Callahan gulps, running a quick hand through his blonde curls.

"Your report, Callahan?" the man barks, his voice gruff and impatient, not bothering to turn round to face the doctor.

"I–I'm afraid they're gone. All of them," Callahan stammers, wiping his clammy palms against his white lab coat. "We have tried to track them, but … we haven't had any luck."

"She's hiding them somewhere." The man clenches his fists. "Everyone else but her is accounted for?"

"Yes, s-sir. It would appear that whoever she was working with isn't part of our team. We think they might be … a journalist."

"A journalist who happens to be able to fly a helicopter?" the man snorts, unconvinced.

"Perhaps a well-connected journalist who *knows* someone that can fly a helicopter," Callahan answers quietly, his head bowed.

"A *journalist*," the man repeats with venom. "What about … the source? What's happened to the magical source?"

Callahan slides his glasses up his nose and braces himself. "It would seem… As far as we can tell… We might be wrong… We're still not—"

"Spit it out, Callahan!" the man bellows.

"It's been destroyed," Callahan squeaks, cowering.

The room falls into silence.

"*Destroyed*?" his companion repeats in disbelief, to be sure he's heard correctly.

"Yes," Callahan confirms, swallowing the lump in his throat.

"On the security footage, it shows her stealing it, not destroying it!"

Callahan grimaces. "I received an email a short while ago with a video of her … blowing it up."

"Videos can be faked!" the man reasons,

desperately clinging to hope.

"I-I've had experts take a look at it," Callahan stammers, wishing he wasn't the one who had to deliver this news. "They're convinced it's real footage."

The man exhales angrily.

"The reason we think she's working with a journalist is because of the email account the video came from," Callahan adds. "It would seem the pseudonym in the email address has been used before to expose certain ... corporate and political scandals. But they've shut that account down now so we were unable to get any further information. Whoever they are, they're good at covering their tracks."

More silence.

Letting his boss process these shocking revelations, Callahan instinctively takes a step backwards towards the exit in case he needs to make a quick escape. But nothing happens and after a while he feels the need to speak.

"W-what would you like us to do?" he asks timidly.

The man takes his time answering, inhaling and

exhaling deeply.

"Shut it down," he orders eventually.

"The project? But s-sir, there's still hope. We could return to the original location where we found the source and try to—"

"I said, *shut it down*," the man seethes. "The entire programme. I want everything destroyed – every last bit of evidence buried."

Shocked, Callahan stands frozen to the spot. So much time and effort has gone into this project. They were unbelievably close to achieving something truly remarkable. To destroy all their work – simply because *she* couldn't see the bigger picture about what they were doing here – was unthinkable! It was wrong! There must be a way the project can be saved!

"We need to shut it down," the man repeats calmly, as though reading his employee's mind. "No one must be able to prove what happened here. Is that understood?"

Disheartened, Callahan's eyes fall to the floor as he whispers, "Yes."

"Good."

Crestfallen, Callahan turns and shuffles to the door, pushing it open.

"Callahan," his boss says suddenly, stopping him.

"Yes?"

"One day, we will find a way to return here. You can rest assured that should that ever be possible, you will have my full financial support. For now, we will abandon this place, but we will not lose sight of our mission. She may have delayed it, but she has not erased it. Remember, the creatures are all out there somewhere. They are the key to our work. When the time is right, when the dust has settled, we will find them. And we will finish what we started. *No one* will get in my way."

A glimmer of hope on the horizon, Callahan leaves the laboratory.

His boss remains behind. His dark, beady eyes scan the cages.

"No one will get in my way," he repeats out loud to the empty room. "Not her. Not *anyone*."

10

# CHAPTER ONE

## Present Day

Today has gone on FOR EVER.

I swear that whenever it's the last day of a school term, time seems to slow down to the point where it almost stops. I've been staring at the clock hanging on the wall behind Mr Leech ALL AFTERNOON and those hands are barely moving.

It doesn't help that Mr Leech is the most boring teacher on the planet. He's leaning back in his chair behind his desk, his hands clasped across his sto͟ droning on about the use of the spinni production of cloth bef

You'd think that it being the final class of the last day before the summer holidays, he might let us watch something instead, but after lunch he announced very clearly that, as far as he was concerned, a school lesson was "for learning" and not "for mucking about".

So, while all the other students in the building are probably being allowed to have fun in the lead up to the final bell, we're stuck here listening to his monotone voice rambling on about YARN.

I sigh heavily, gazing out of the window at the school sports field, losing myself in a daydream about what I'm going to do this summer. Not much, is the answer. But that's OK. Anything is better than school. I'm sure Dad has planned some days out for us. During the last school holidays, he took some days off work and we went camping, which was so much fun. We did bike rides through the woods, toasted marshmallows on the campfire and told each ~~other~~ ghost stories.

~~I wonder i~~f he'll be able to take some time ~~off work this~~ summer. He works in marketing and has been so busy recently that he's had to commute to London much more than usual. We live a few hours away from the city – whenever he has to go there for the day, he's exhausted by the time he gets back. Like yesterday, when I had to go to our next-door neighbour Robin's house for tea because Dad didn't get home until nine o'clock.

It doesn't bother me that Dad has to work a lot, but in the holidays it can get a bit lonely when he's out all the time. This is why I keep pestering him to get me a dog, because then I'd have a companion and Dad wouldn't have to worry about me at all. But whenever I put forward my well-thought-out and persuasive argument, he raises his eyebrows at me and goes, "Nice try, kid," with this knowing smile. I don't know what's so amusing. I'm being serious. I'll wear him down one day about getting a dog. The trick is to pester him when he's trying to watch the football, as he may just say yes to get me to go away and leave him in peace.

Of course, Dad would prefer that I hang out with

friends rather than a pet. But there's one problem with that: I don't have any.

"LUNA WOLF!"

I jump at my name. Mr Leech is glaring at me from his desk and my cheeks grow hot under the attention as everyone in the class swivels in their seats to look in my direction.

"S-sorry, Mr Leech," I stutter, quickly looking down at my open textbook. "What was the question?"

There's a ripple of sniggers through the class.

"There *wasn't* a question," he corrects me huffily. "I was checking to see if you were listening, and it is quite obvious that you were not! Do you think I'm sitting here, teaching you about the Industrial Revolution for my own amusement?"

Nervously fiddling with my necklace, I shake my head.

"No," he barks, shifting in his seat. "Now, if you wouldn't mind, please do us all the honour of *paying attention*."

He clears his throat and returns to his monologue

while I sink down lower in my seat, my face feeling like it's on fire. Thankfully, everyone else has returned to pretending to listen and I'm no longer under their scrutinizing gaze. I watch as Melanie Caramel, who sits a couple of rows in front, turns her back to me again, flicking her glossy chestnut-brown hair over her shoulder and going back to scrolling through her phone under her desk. She's the most popular girl in our class. I bet Melanie Caramel has AMAZING plans for the summer. I bet she is going somewhere really hot and sunny and glamorous, and her big group of friends is probably going there too. I reckon they've got lots of parties at each other's houses lined up as well, so every weekend from now until September is booked out.

My heart sinks as I compare my summer to my idea of Melanie Caramel's. I've never been good at making friends. It's like everyone but me was given a code about fitting in. My school reports have always said the same thing: *quiet, keeps herself to herself, doesn't speak up enough in class.*

It's not like I'm shy on purpose. I have tried to make friends before, but it never goes well. Like the time I tried to join in on a conversation that Melanie Caramel was having over lunch with her friends about her parents going to Canada to visit family. I overheard and realized that I might be able to impress her with my knowledge about the grizzly bears who live there.

That very morning, Dad had gently said to me that I should try putting myself out there a bit more with my classmates, because in his opinion, I was the "greatest girl in the world" and there was no way that people wouldn't want to be friends with me once they had the chance to get to know me.

So, I decided to take his advice and try to join in. Big mistake.

"Your parents might see some bears," I told Melanie excitedly, leaning towards her with enthusiasm, my contribution to the conversation taking her by surprise. "There are three species of bear native to Canada: the grizzly, the black bear and the polar.

16

If your family lives on the West Coast, then your parents will hopefully see a grizzly! Although I think the black bear is the most common one out there."

"Aren't grizzly bears and black bears the same thing?" one of Melanie's friends, Ella, asked, frowning at me in confusion.

"No, grizzly bears have brown fur," I informed her happily. "Similar to the colour of your hair, Melanie!"

Melanie wrinkled her nose at me in disgust. "Are you saying I look like a *bear*?"

"No! No, of course not!" I squeaked, mortified.

But the damage was done. She pointedly stood up, picked up her lunch tray and marched out of the canteen, followed by all her friends, each of them giving me a dirty look.

That was the last time I spoke to Melanie Caramel. When my dad picked me up from school that afternoon, he asked how my day had been and looked very confused when I told him that my attempt at making friends had led to me accidentally likening the most popular girl in school to a Canadian grizzly bear.

I've accepted that I'm not going to make any friends at school any time soon and I should be content with my own company. I just need to keep my head down and not get in anyone's way. I have to be invisible. That's the best way to get through the day.

And maybe this summer, I could try to volunteer at Hobble Farm, even though they keep telling me I'm too young. Hobble Farm is a few minutes' bike ride from our house and it's open all summer for people to come and see the animals. I've applied there a few times, but the manager says that he cannot let a twelve-year-old help out, even though I've told him I'm happy to muck out the horses, feed the pigs and the goats, whatever he needs! It hasn't worked: the answer is still no. I'll try again, just in case.

I'd be much happier hanging out with all the animals there than with anyone from school. Dad says I get that from Mum. She was amazing with animals. She was a scientist and did all this groundbreaking research into veterinary medicines and healthcare. Dad has told me that she had this incredibly calm, gentle aura, and animals were just drawn to her, naturally at ease in her company. They knew that they could trust her.

I have a lot of precious memories that I try to cling on to of being with her at places like Hobble Farm. I remember her holding me up in  her arms so I could stroke the horses' noses, and I remember her giggling with me as I let the horses nibble at my palm as they searched for more sugar lumps. I remember the farm dogs – three or four Border collies at a time – always running towards her as soon as she got out of the car, and jumping all over her, trying to lick her face. She wouldn't hesitate to get down on her knees in the mud to give them all cuddles and fuss.

We have a photo on our fridge that Dad took of me and Mum with those dogs. She's crouching next to me, a huge smile on her face, her blue necklace glinting in the sunshine, the two of us laughing, surrounded by dogs.

That was the picture they chose to print in the local newspaper two years ago when they turned one of the unused fields at Hobble Farm into a wild meadow, and they asked Dad's permission to name it after her because she helped them out so much with their animals for free. Even when she was sick herself, she would still visit poorly pets and animals in the area to see if she could help. The headline in the paper ran:

# ATHENA'S MEADOW FINISHED

Meadow of colourful wildflowers named after
late pioneering animal scientist

*Athena's Meadow.* She would have loved that.

I also remember her telling me stories at bedtime

about all the amazing animals she was surrounded by when she was growing up in Jamaica: the colourful birds, the serene sea turtles, the busy lizards. Dad says that she once bought me a storybook about a Jamaican iguana, and I loved it so much that I refused to put it down and carried the book everywhere with me. It was my version of a safety blanket. According to him, Mum found that hilarious and beamed with pride about it, telling everyone that I was following in her footsteps.

Thinking about Mum makes me instinctively fidget with my necklace. It's the blue one from the photo, the one that she never took off. When she died five years ago, Dad gave it to me. It's a simple gold chain with a small, jagged blue pendant. I never take it off, ever. I know it sounds silly, but this necklace makes me feel connected to her somehow.

I wish I could remember more about her.

"LUNA WOLF!" Mr Leech bellows again, jolting me from my thoughts about Mum. "If I catch you in a daydream one more time, I am going to—"

*BRRRRR-IIIIIING!*

I am, quite literally, saved by the bell. The sound of chair legs scraping along the floor fills the room as everyone in the class jumps to their feet in excitement. It's officially the summer holidays. Mr Leech gives a heavy sigh and, as my classmates busily shove their belongings into their bags and rush towards the door, he attempts to remind us above the din to complete our assigned summer reading.

Closing my textbook and sliding it into my bag, I gingerly stand up and shuffle after the rest of the class towards the exit, avoiding eye contact with him.

"Miss Wolf," he says as I reach the door, forcing me to turn round to face him. "May I suggest that before September, you spend some time working on improving your attention span? I would hate for you to start the new school year off on the wrong foot."

"Will do, Mr Leech," I reply quietly, before adding, "at least you won't have to put up with me any more, since I'll have a new teacher," in an attempt to lighten the mood.

He narrows his eyes at me. "Actually, it's been decided that from September I'll also be teaching year eight. I'll be your form tutor. See you next term."

I grimace, turning away from him and hurrying out of there as quickly as possible. Another year of Mr Leech and his droning?! UGH!

Slinging my backpack over my shoulder, I join the chattering, bustling crowd of students making their way towards the exit of our school building. Stepping out into the sunshine, I scan the sea of parents waiting at the gates to pick up their kids and brighten as I spot Dad lurking at the back. He catches my eye and his face lights up as he holds up his hands to show me that he's carrying two small tubs of ice cream from our favourite vegan gelato shop on the high street.

Dodging through the crowd, I run towards him and give him a hug.

"Hey, Luna." He laughs as I throw my arms around his waist. "Happy summer holidays! I got you your favourite flavour to celebrate."

"Chocolate with extra chocolate chips!" I grin,

23

gratefully taking my tub from him.

He chuckles, putting his arm around my shoulders and guiding me away from the gates as we start our walk home. We live a twenty-minute walk from the school, which in the summer is a quiet stroll down the high street and then along a couple of fields to our house at the end of a lane. But when the weather is not so nice, we do the school run in the car, and it only takes about five minutes. Today, I'm happy to walk in the sun, relishing the free time that's stretching out ahead of me, and trying not to worry about spending that time feeling a bit lonely.

"So, how was your day?" Dad asks.

"Horrible," I say through a mouthful of ice cream. "Mr Leech kept yelling at me."

"Daydreaming again?"

I shrug. "I wouldn't daydream so much if he didn't talk so much."

"He's your teacher." Dad laughs. "He's supposed to talk."

"How was your day?"

"It was … good," Dad says, frowning slightly and looking distracted.

"What's wrong?" I ask, watching his expression closely.

"Nothing, nothing," he replies quickly with a wave of his hand. He focuses his attention back on his ice cream. "This ice cream isn't bad, is it?"

"It's the best."

"I'm not so sure," he contends. "There's a vegan gelato place in London that I visited yesterday, and I think it's even better than this."

"You went to a gelato shop without me?" I gasp, pretending to be insulted. "How could you?"

"I figured you'd forgive me if I bought you a couple of scoops today," he says, nodding to the tub in my hands, which is already almost empty.

"Seriously, though, Luna, the gelato in London is much better."

"I'll believe that when I taste it. I meant to ask you, did you see Nan yesterday?"

"Actually, I did. She was asking after you. She misses you a lot."

"I miss her," I say, finishing my last mouthful of ice cream and throwing the tub in a bin as we pass.

Nan is my mum's mum and lives in Tottenham in North London. We see her as often as we can, and she often comes here to Wiltshire to spend weekends with us. Whenever she arrives, she talks about how wonderful it is to be in the countryside, how the air is so clean and how peaceful it is. But by the end of the weekend, she's complaining that it's too eerily quiet and that she doesn't know how we can put up with the constant smell of cowpat that burns her nostrils, and we all know she's itching to get back to London. Dad and I love that about her – Nan is warm and fun and the best hostess in the world. Her cooking is second to none and her dishes of stew, pea soup and Jamaican fruit cake are famous on her road. Her neighbours are always popping in when she's cooking something up in the hope of being asked to stay for dinner, which they can guarantee they will be because Nan isn't one to turn anybody away.

When Mum died, Nan came here for a few weeks to take care of us, insisting on helping Dad even though he was trying to make out like he could cope on his own. He wasn't coping, though, he admits. I remember Nan being like a bolt of colour through the dark sadness of that time, bustling around our house, tidying and making sure everything was in order and sparkling clean, filling our fridge with food, and taking me out on daily adventures so Dad could have some time on his own.

I know now that taking me out on those walks, during which I'd drag her towards any farm animals we passed on the way, wouldn't exactly have been her idea of fun. She doesn't mind animals, but she HATES any kind of mess – her house in London is pristine. And, in her mind, animals equal mess.

I like when we travel to London to see Nan, but sometimes she'll invite all her side of the family over for dinner so that everyone can catch up, and that kind of situation makes me nervous. I find it a bit loud and overwhelming, especially as I'll be the centre of attention, and they'll ask me loads of questions. I prefer it when it's just me, Dad and Nan. Sometimes, when it's just us three, Nan will tell me stories about Mum, and I love hearing about her. Dad doesn't talk about Mum too often. I think he finds it too painful.

"How is she?" I ask Dad as we turn down a country lane towards home.

"Hmm?" he replies, his mind elsewhere. "Who?"

"Nan!"

"Oh! She's fine. She's good. She's great." He swirls his ice cream around the tub with his spoon, having barely made a dent in it.

"Dad, what's wrong?" I ask, stopping and putting my hands on my hips.

"Nothing's wrong!" he insists.

"You're acting weird. Are you worried about me and the summer holidays? Because I've told you that I'm absolutely fine. You don't need to worry about entertaining me."

"No, no, I'm not worried about *that*," he says.

"Well, something is wrong." I cross my arms stubbornly. "Come on, Dad, tell me what's going on."

He breathes out slowly. "OK," he says, giving in. "I want to talk to you about something. I have ... some news. I was going to wait until we got home, but I suppose I might as well tell you now."

"I'm listening."

He offers me a weak smile. "Luna, I've been offered a promotion at work."

"Dad! That's great!"

"Yes." He nods. "But it'll mean longer hours and many more meetings in London."

"So, you'd be commuting there every day?"

"Not exactly. We ... we're moving to London. Me and you. In just over a week's time."

I blink at him, stunned, not sure what to say.

"It's a fantastic opportunity and I really do want the job. I've spoken to Nan about it, and she's offered to have us stay with her for a while until we find our own place to live." He peers at me, scrutinizing my expression. "Are you OK? Talk to me."

"Yeah," I say, swallowing the lump in my throat. "I'm just … we're moving to London?"

"If you're happy to," he says quickly, watching me with concern. "And … well … that's not my only piece of news. There's another reason I would like us to move to London, Luna."

"What is it?"

"I've met someone," he admits quietly, his eyes glistening as he smiles hopefully at me. "I've met someone special."

# CHAPTER TWO

A new adventure.

That's how Dad keeps describing it. A new adventure for both of us. An exciting, fresh start. New surroundings, new people, new city, new school, new *everything*.

He's very excited about it. Ever since he broke the news to me a week ago, it's like a weight has been lifted off his shoulders. He's tackling chores in such a positive and upbeat manner, it's unnerving: he shimmies around the kitchen when he cooks; he hums happily while he does the washing-up; he tangos with the hoover; he giggles, popping bits of bubble wrap as he packs our belongings. He's suddenly so … *happy*.

He keeps asking me how I feel about it all.

The truth is, I don't know how I feel.

For the first couple of days, I think I was in shock. It's such a big change and, for me, it's come out of nowhere. I didn't know Dad was interested in ever living in a city. And I had NO idea that he was dating. He's never shown any enthusiasm for dating since Mum died. I was completely unprepared. Lucy is the special someone he's met, and he keeps apologizing for not telling me about her before now. His excuse was that he hadn't been looking to meet someone, it "just sort of happened", and then he didn't want to bother me with the news until he was sure it was serious. Before he knew it, it was very serious, and he was desperate for me to meet her.

Her and her son.

Yeah, another little nugget of information that Dad threw in there on that fateful last school day when he revealed all his secrets that were going to change my life for ever. My dad's new girlfriend Lucy has a son called Kieron, who's my age. Apparently, they're both certain that we're going to get on really well.

This is a classic parent mistake: just because we're the same age won't automatically make us friends. Considering I've had zero luck making friends with anyone my own age so far, I doubt that anything will be different with Kieron.

I feel sick when I think about being forced to hang out with Lucy and Kieron. I feel terrified at the idea of living in a brand-new place. I feel overwhelmed by all this change.

But I also feel a teeny-tiny glimmer of hope. Maybe this *will* be a big adventure and a fresh start for me. School can't be any worse there than it is here. I won't have to listen to Mr Leech's lectures ever again. Melanie Caramel and her snooty friends will be a distant memory. I'll have the chance to start again. I'll meet new people and *maybe* make friends.

Sometimes, when I'm thinking along those lines, I let myself feel a little bit excited about the move. After all, it's nice to see Dad this happy again. It's great he got a promotion. He deserves it after working so hard. And, yeah, it may be weird to see him with someone who isn't Mum, but it's been several years since she died, and I know how lost he's been without her. I don't want him to be alone for ever.

Although, it's been just me and Dad for so long. The two of us against the world. No one gets me like he does. I don't know how it's going to be with Lucy and Kieron coming into the picture too. Will my relationship with Dad change? He's already so busy with work, will he still have time for me when he's juggling a new relationship? Or will everything be about Lucy now? Will she expect to just waltz into my life and be my *mother*? Because I do NOT need a new one. I already have one, thank you very much, so she'd better not think I'm going to let her boss me around and tell me what to do. Will she want me to call her "Mum"? Is that what Dad wants? UGH.

And what if she hates me? It's not like I'm the life and soul of the party. If Melanie Caramel is to be believed, I'm a freak. A loser. Lucy might not like losers. And then because she doesn't like me, maybe Dad will stop liking me. Maybe he'll take her side. Maybe he'll prefer her son to me.

The new people at my new school probably won't like losers, either. I'll be as big an outcast as ever, but in a scary city I don't know without Hobble Farm to escape to! This move is surely more likely to be a total disaster than an exciting new adventure.

And what about Athena's Meadow? It's named after Mum, and now we're moving away. I get that it's a field and it's not actually Mum, but for some reason I feel weirdly guilty about not living down the road from somewhere so special to our family.

So, you can see why, when my mind starts to spiral like this, it's difficult to give Dad a straight answer when he asks me, "How do you feel about it all?"

"Fine, Dad," I tend to say.

But that's a lie. I don't feel fine at all.

Nan is standing outside her front door when we

pull up in the car on a sunny Saturday morning. She's wearing a bright orange dress, green-framed sunglasses and large gold earrings that glint in the sunlight when she moves her head. When I step out of the car, she breaks into a wide grin and throws open her arms to envelop me in a big hug.

"I've missed you, Luna," she says, putting her hands on my arms as I pull back so she can take me in properly. "You've grown again!"

I instinctively drop my eyes to the ground. One of the tallest in my class, I've felt self-conscious about my height for a while now, hunching on purpose and wishing I was shorter and less visible so I could blend in more. Nan reaches out and lifts my chin with her finger.

"You're going to be strikingly tall, just like your mother. Beautiful. Commanded the attention of any room she walked into."

"I'm not sure I want to command any attention," I admit shyly.

Nan chuckles. "Ah, she was the same. But sometimes people are born to stand out, and you, my Luna, are one of those people. I can tell. You shouldn't be bashful about what makes you special. Your height comes from our side of the family – one of your great-uncles was so tall that he once caught a parrot in mid-air! Swept it right out of the sky!"

I burst out laughing. Nan is always telling outrageous stories and, despite her insistence that they're all true, I'm not sure I believe her. Dad says when Mum brought him home for the first time to meet Nan, he felt the same about her stories, including one about Mum's cousin, whom Nan claimed had such a strong forehead that he could crack a melon in half with one headbutt. Apparently, Dad laughed at the "nonsense" story and received such a sharp glare from Nan that he stopped laughing straight away and decided that he'd believe every story she ever told him for the rest of time.

Having once been on the receiving end of one of Nan's discerning looks myself – when I stuck my finger in the bowl of sauce she was making before she'd given me permission – I can confirm that you

NEVER want her to look at you that way.

I swear, she could make the most powerful person in the world break out into a sweat with just one look. Everyone in our family knows: you do not mess with Nan.

"You are very welcome here," Nan announces, ushering Dad over for a hug too, as he lugs a suitcase out of the car and up to her front door. "How was the drive? Richard, you haven't been eating well; you're working too hard, aren't you? What have I told you about the importance of diet? It fuels the brain. Come inside; let's get you settled. I hope you packed your shirts better than the last time you stayed here; thrown into the suitcase without a thought, all crumpled and creased."

Dad rolls his eyes behind her back, but it's obvious he secretly loves it when she bosses him about. I know he's already feeling right at home. I never knew Dad's parents, as they died before I was born, and he was an only child, so he doesn't have any family. When he and Mum got married, her family became his family and Nan treats him like her son, scolding him and fussing over him.

I head back to the car to grab some bags. Most of our things have gone into storage until we have our own house to move into, so I only packed what I'd need for the summer. Careful to wipe my shoes on the doormat, I follow Dad into the house and am instructed by Nan to put my bags in my "usual room" upstairs, which is Mum's old bedroom, right at the far end of the landing. Dad and Nan's voices drift up the stairs as they chat away in the kitchen, and I smile to myself as I overhear him assuring her that he had a cup of tea from a service station on the way. She replies that she'll make him a hot drink because the standard of tea they serve in those places is "disgraceful".

Dropping my bags in the middle of Mum's bedroom, I sit down on the edge of the single bed next to the window and look around at my new home for the next couple of months. As ever, the bed has been perfectly made, with not one crease in the duvet and with several plump cushions arranged up against the pillows. It's very tidy in here, no clutter anywhere. There's nothing on Mum's old desk in the corner, and I bet if I open the wardrobe and the chest of drawers, they'll be empty too, ready for me to fill.

I only notice one thing that's changed since the last time I stayed here: on the bedside table, there's a photo frame that wasn't there before. I pick it up

to look at it properly. It's a picture of Mum. She's wearing her lab coat, and her hand is resting on the head of what looks like a gorgeous long-legged, muscly white dog with some caramel-coloured splodges on his back, who is facing away from the camera. Mum is laughing, looking down at the dog, and I assume that she was trying to get him to look the right way for the picture and failing miserably.

My hand instinctively flying to my necklace

pendant, I examine the picture closely, peering through the glass of the frame as I try to work out where it was taken. She's standing in front of a grey steel building that I don't recognize.

"I found that picture the other day."

I snap my head up at Nan's voice. She is watching me from the doorway, smiling warmly.

"I haven't seen it before," I admit, admiring the picture again. "Was this where she worked?"

"Yes, I think so. Before you moved to the countryside."

"Whose dog is this?"

Nan chuckles, shaking her head. "Who knows? Your mum was always rescuing waifs and strays."

"I don't remember having a dog when I was little."

"You didn't," she says, coming over to sit next to me on the bed and looking over my shoulder at the photo. "Your mum was too busy with work to have a dog, as much as she wanted one. This must have been a colleague's dog, or perhaps one of the animals she was helping with her medicines."

"So many of the photos I've seen of Mum have a dog in them too."

"Mmm. She had a bond with animals. You should have heard her when she was your age, begging me for a dog. I told her that it would be me doing all the work: picking up after it, cleaning up after it, walking it! But she was adamant she'd do all of that."

"You still didn't give in?"

She raises her eyebrows at me. "What do you think?"

I laugh. "I guess she couldn't take a dog to school with her."

"Certainly not. But that didn't stop her pestering me every single day." She fondly gazes down at Mum's smiling face. "She was very determined your mother. When she had an idea in her head, there was nothing that could stop her. If she couldn't have a dog at home, then she was going to forge herself a career where she could be with dogs at work."

I place the frame carefully back on the bedside table.

"I wish I could be more like her," I say out loud without thinking.

"You're more like her than you realize," Nan insists, nudging my arm with hers.

I smile at her gratefully, and then we're both distracted by Dad's wheezing and puffing as he drags his suitcase up the stairs, stopping at the top and wiping his brow. He notices us watching him through the open door and his expression brightens.

"How would you feel about checking out the local area, Luna?" he suggests. "I thought we could go for a little explore and get some of that gelato I told you about."

"Excellent idea," Nan says, getting to her feet and encouraging me to follow suit. "You can pop to the shop and pick up a few things for me. I need to start preparing food tonight before they all descend on the house tomorrow!"

My eyes widen in panic. "*They*? What's happening tomorrow?"

"Our big family dinner!" she says joyfully. "They're all coming here to welcome you to the city and to celebrate this next chapter in your life."

I had been hoping it would be just us three for the

weekend. I should have known Nan would organize a big do for us. I love the wider family, but whenever we see them it's a really big deal because they all live in London and see each other all the time, so the attention is always on me and Dad. It's hard to be safely invisible when you have to answer a billion questions about your life.

I'm wondering how I can possibly get out of it, when Nan throws in another startling suggestion. "Richard, you must invite Lucy and Kieron to join us too."

"Oh, I don't know about that," Dad says quickly, his eyebrows knitting together in concern as he looks at me. "We can stick with family."

"Nonsense!" Nan says stubbornly. "They are very welcome. It will be nice for Luna to get to know them! Lucy is lovely and I would like to meet Kieron."

"Wait, you've already met Lucy?" I ask, confused.

"Very briefly, which is why it would be nice to have her over, so I can speak to her for longer than two minutes," Nan explains. "She runs the animal rescue centre around the corner, and I met her a year ago when there was a stray dog in the area. He was sitting right on my doorstep, so I gave the shelter a call and she came to pick him up. He was a tough cookie that dog, it took her a while to get him to move from my drive!"

"Lucy runs a rescue centre?" I turn to Dad in surprise. "You didn't tell me that."

He sighs. "Because I knew that as soon as I did, you'd start pestering me for one of the dogs that she looks after."

"Ah," Nan says, giving me a knowing smile. "Now that sounds like a familiar story."

## *Seven Years Ago: Before The Escape*

"Ready?" Joanna asks, lifting the camera. "Try to get him to look this way."

"I'm trying." Athena giggles, crouching next to the dog and attempting to encourage him to look in Joanna's direction. "Come on, silly boy, pose for the picture."

Instead, the dog gives her a big lick across the face. Athena bursts out laughing and hears a click as Joanna takes the shot. She lowers the camera, shaking her head as the dog remains determined to look back at the large grey steel warehouse behind them, distracted by whatever might be happening over there.

"They do say never to work with animals," Joanna reasons with a shrug.

Athena sighs, straightening and patting the dog on the head. "Oh well, we'll have to try to get a nice photo another day. Thanks for your help."

Passing the camera back to Athena, Joanna smiles, pleased to be helpful. As one of the junior scientists working on the project, she looks up to Athena and likes gaining her approval. Joanna is always a bit embarrassed by the fact that most people on the team – including that dreary Dr Callahan – think she only got the job because of her father. Athena never makes her feel that way. Athena's belief in Joanna helps her to believe in herself.

"You won't tell anyone about taking this picture, will you?" Athena says, winking at her as they wander back towards the warehouse entrance. "You know what the boss says: no photo evidence of the animals."

"I won't say anything, I promise," Joanna replies. "I don't know why Dad has made that rule. It seems silly."

Athena shrugs. "I'm sure he has his reasons. But

I wanted at least one picture of my boy." She smiles down at the dog trotting along next to her. "Not that he was even looking at the camera!"

"Dr Wolf!" a voice barks from the doorway of the warehouse.

Athena looks up to see Callahan waiting for her.

"There you are," he says as the two women approach, running his thumb and forefinger along his thick moustache. "What were you doing out here?"

"Getting some fresh air," Athena replies calmly. "Joanna and I were having a chat."

"I should be in Lab Three," Joanna says, shuffling away. "See you later."

Plastering a smile on his face, Callahan gives her a cheery wave, before he and Athena make their way to the doors past reception.

"She's already made three mistakes today that I've had to cover up," Callahan mutters, his expression falling as soon as Joanna has disappeared through the doors ahead of them. "She shouldn't be working on this project. It's too important."

"Those feelings don't seem to stop you from sucking up to her," Athena observes with a sly smile. "You should try not to think of her as the boss's daughter – she needs to know about her mistakes so she can learn from them."

Callahan holds open the door for her, raising his eyebrows at the dog remaining stuck to her side as she strolls through.

"I don't know why you bother to take them out of the lab," he sneers. "They're not pets."

"They are to me, and I enjoy making sure they have a happy, healthy life," Athena says stubbornly. "We have a special bond with these animals."

Callahan snorts, a flash of irritation clouding features. "*You* have a special bond."

"Give it time. Once we've done some more research into the source and things are a bit clearer, I'm sure you can—"

"Get more involved, yes, yes." Callahan sighs impatiently. "You keep saying this."

Athena presses her lips together, not saying

anything as she follows him down the corridor towards the main laboratory. She reaches out and stops him just as they reach the double doors at the end.

"Callahan, wait. I've been meaning to talk to you for a while."

He puts his hands in his pockets. "About what?"

She hesitates. "Is ... is there something you're not telling me about this project?"

He frowns at her. "What are you talking about?"

"This morning I saw you and the boss whispering together, and then you sprang apart as soon as I came over. I don't know, but sometimes I get the feeling that" – she pauses, searching for the right words – "you're hiding something from me."

He shifts uncomfortably. "Don't be absurd."

"He's been vague about plans for the future, and I see you two talking conspiratorially together all the time," Athena says, scrutinizing his expression as he avoids eye contact with her. "There are secret files I'm not allowed access to, but you are – even though, technically, I'm heading up this project. If there's something I should know—"

"You're imagining things," he snaps, cutting her off.

The dog at Athena's feet growls threateningly at him.

"We have to get back to work," Callahan concludes, scowling at the dog as he pushes open the doors to the lab and marches in, immediately barking orders at the rest of their team.

It doesn't matter what Callahan says, Athena can't shake the feeling that there's more to this project than she's been told. And that doesn't sit well with her, not when the lives of such beautiful creatures are at stake. She places a comforting hand on the head of the dog as he nuzzles against her leg.

Whatever secret Callahan is hiding, she's going to uncover it.

# CHAPTER THREE

## *Present Day*

I've only been in London a day and I already feel completely lost.

There are so many people here, and it's noisy and busy and ... terrifying. Nan says those are all the things that give the city its bright, colourful personality, but I'm not so sure. Where Nan lives is pretty residential and quiet, but when we walked to the park yesterday, there was so much traffic on the roads, everyone beeping impatiently, and I felt like I got in everyone's way at the shop we visited to pick up ingredients for the family dinner.

Today, Dad thought it would be a fun idea to go into Central London to see some of the sights and the tube was sweltering, and I didn't understand the map at all. Dad laughed when I said that as we hurtled down the Victoria line, and he told me not to worry and I'd get the hang of it eventually. As I tripped over someone's foot, before knocking into someone else's shoulder in an attempt to get off the train, I thought to myself that I'm not sure I *want* to get the hang of it.

I think it's best if I stay in the safety of my bedroom, out of the way. I suppose in such a big city with so many people, it will be easier to be invisible here than my old home anyway, which could be a good thing. It's not like I ever felt like I belonged there, either.

I wish I could hide away in my bedroom for tonight too. I can hear Nan downstairs in the kitchen, singing along to Beres Hammond as she whips up a variety of delicious dishes. The smells wafting up the stairs are already making my mouth water. But then I remember all the people coming and I don't feel so hungry any more. I can't believe I'm going to meet Lucy and Kieron. I'm still trying to get my head round the idea of my dad even having a girlfriend, and now I'm having to spend the evening with her and her son.

When we were walking down The Mall towards Buckingham Palace earlier today, Dad did make a point of checking whether I was happy for them to join us for dinner.

"It's completely up to you," he said, looking at me apprehensively. "At Nan's insistence I have invited them, and Lucy has said they'd love to meet you, but I appreciate that this is all new for you, and you might want some more time to settle in before you meet them. So, if you're uncomfortable with them being there tonight, don't be afraid to tell me – just say the word and we can meet them another time. They'll understand."

I didn't say anything at first, looking down at the ground as we walked. If I was honest with myself, it did feel a bit soon when we'd only arrived in the city yesterday, but then I figured it might be better to meet them in a crowd rather than when it's just the four of us. That way, I won't be stuck being forced to talk to them all evening, because there'll be lots of other people to distract them. With my family there to chat away with them, it will be a little less intense for me.

So, I lifted my chin, offered him a small smile and said, "Thanks, Dad, but I'm fine with them coming to dinner this evening."

He put his arm around me, squeezed me tight, and then, maybe sensing that a change of subject might be a good idea to lighten the mood, launched into a history lesson about the royal family as we approached the black iron gates of the palace.

"Luna!" Nan calls up the stairs now as I sit on the bed, hugging my knees to my chest. "Come help me stir the soup please! Everyone will be arriving any minute!"

With a heavy sigh, I force myself to stand and drag my feet to the door, shuffling across the landing and plodding down the stairs. Nan looks up as I appear in the kitchen doorway and grins at me.

"Here," she says, ushering me over to the pot. "You keep stirring that and then you can help me get all the cutlery ready. We'll eat out in the garden. It's such a lovely evening."

I nod, taking the spoon and getting to work.

"How was your day out?" Nan asks, as she focuses her attention on cutting the hardo bread.

"Fine," I shrug.

"It's a big place, London. Give yourself time to find your feet. When I first came here, I didn't know what to do with myself. A big, scary city like this – the lifestyle is very different to what I was used to. But sometimes you need a push out of your comfort zone to face up to your fears and find yourself."

"Did Mum fit in straight away when you moved here?"

"Oh yes." She nods. "But your mum could fit in anywhere. You're a bit more reserved, like your father. I always liked that about him – he took time to come out of his shell, but when he did, the family all adored him. Not easy to meet a big family like ours, is it?"

"I guess."

"Did you go to the animal shelter yesterday on your way to the shops?"

"We passed it."

"Don't you go getting any ideas," Nan says, waggling her finger at me. "No animals will be allowed to live here, is that clear? Tina, who lives two doors down, let her daughter get a hamster. The creature escaped its hutch and used her brand-new corner sofa as a toilet! I refuse to deal with droppings."

"Don't worry, Nan. I won't be getting a hamster any time soon."

"No rodents under this roof. And no dogs or cats for that matter, either. Your cousin Clive rescued a puppy and I've never seen so much fur on an animal! He had to buy a new vacuum to cope."

"Some dogs don't moult."

She raises her eyebrows at me. "You think those dogs don't have paws either, hmm? You think they don't splash through muddy puddles and then run about your carpets? You think they won't slobber at the whiff of the Ackee and Saltfish and leave a puddle of drool on my kitchen floor, ready for me to slip in and break my arm? Luna Wolf, if you think I haven't heard every argument under the sun about the advantages of dogs from your mother, then you are mistaken."

The doorbell goes and Nan's face lights up. "Ah! They are on time! I suppose there's a first for everything."

As she hurries out of the kitchen to get the door and Dad's footsteps rush down the stairs to join her in greeting everyone, I nervously hide back in the kitchen, busying myself with my stirring. There's an eruption of noise as Nan opens the door, and my aunts, uncles and several cousins say their hellos and burst into the house, all of them speaking over each other as they tell Dad how good it is to see him and how well he looks, before immediately demanding to know where I am.

I meekly step away from the hob and give them a

wave from the kitchen doorway, prompting a further outburst of joyful greetings as they come hurrying towards me, and I find myself lost in a throng of hugs. Flushing at the attention, I try to take in the torrent of questions that keep coming, despite receiving no answers because I can't get a word in edgeways. Aunty Gracie tells me I have the exact same eyes as Mum, while Aunty Shirley says no, I have her smile, and Uncle Desmond says I've grown twice the size in just a year.

My cousins are all carrying various dishes they've brought for the meal and start asking where to put them, their parents telling them to set them down on the counters or on the table, which prompts further commotion when Nan comes in and tells all of them off for messing up her organized kitchen, instructing them to move the dishes to the table outside. As they pour into the garden, I head to the cutlery drawer and begin to count out the number of knives and forks we're going to need, thankful for the quiet as their conversations continue outdoors.

The noise of their entrance clearly drowned out the doorbell ringing a second time, because I turn round to see Dad stepping into the kitchen, followed by a woman, who is holding a bouquet of flowers, and a boy. The woman is just shorter than Dad and has dark wavy hair and sharp cheekbones, with large brown eyes and bold red lipstick that matches the bright red dress she's paired with a waistcoat. She's very striking. The boy wearing a T-shirt and navy-blue shorts and standing awkwardly next to her, has her brown eyes and dark eyelashes behind black-framed glasses, and unruly black curly hair. His eyebrows are knitted together as he glances up at me, and then he looks back down at the floor.

He looks as though he wants to be here as much as I do.

"Luna," Dad begins, taking a deep breath and gesturing at the two of them. "I'd like you to meet Lucy and Kieron."

Lucy smiles warmly at me. "Hi, Luna, I've heard so much about you," she says. "It's great to finally meet!"

I can't exactly say *I've heard so much about you too*, because that would be a lie, so instead I keep my distance on the other side of the kitchen, and I offer her a half-hearted wave, lifting my hand and dropping it again.

"Kieron is in the same school year as you," Dad says brightly, as though that means anything.

I nod. Kieron shoves his hands in his shorts' pockets.

When neither of us says anything else, Dad and

Lucy share a look, both of them desperately searching for a prompt as to what to do next.

"There you are," Nan says, returning from ordering everyone about outside just in time to rescue the situation. "Ah, Lucy! How lovely to see you again; you're very welcome! And this must be Kieron. You look just like your mum!"

"Hi, Clementine," Lucy says with a smile of relief at the interruption. She holds out the flowers to Nan. "These are for you. Thank you for having us."

"How beautiful! Thank you! I'll get these in some water right away so they don't wilt in this heat. You can go out into the garden – Richard, why don't you do the introductions, and I'll keep Luna and Kieron busy in here? Kieron, can you get me a vase from the cupboard there to your left? Thank you."

With a grateful look to Nan, Dad gestures for Lucy to head outside, leaving Kieron and I at her mercy. Kieron sets about finding a suitable vase for the flowers they've brought, while I continue counting the knives and forks.

"Do you like cooking, Kieron?" Nan asks, having requested that we linger in the kitchen to help her carry the food out once it's ready.

He shakes his head. "Not really."

"Luna has no interest in it, either," she informs him, rolling her eyes. "When I was your age, I loved helping my parents in the kitchen! My father made a mean curry."

"Is that how you learned to cook?" Kieron asks, watching her dole out spoonfuls of rice and peas. "From your parents?"

"Oh yes, I learned everything from them." Nan smiles. "Are you good with animals like your mum?"

He shrugs. "Sort of. I help Mum out at the rescue centre sometimes."

"That's very good! You know, Luna here is very interested in animals. Aren't you, Luna?"

I keep my eyes focused on the cutlery. I know what Nan is doing and it's not going to work. She can't *force* us to be friends.

"Do you want to work with animals when you're

older?" Nan asks Kieron, giving up on waiting for me to speak.

"No, I'd like to be a journalist," he says firmly, sliding his glasses up his nose. "An investigative journalist."

"Wow!" Nan says, impressed, handing him the salad servers and pointing at the salad bowl and the dressing beside it so he knows to start mixing.

"I've written lots of articles already," Kieron says pompously. "I have my own blog."

"How wonderful," Nan enthuses.

"If only something interesting would happen here, but the rescue centre isn't exactly the place to go for breaking news." He sighs, rolling his eyes. "It's pretty boring there. Just a load of dogs and cats."

I shoot him a glare, which neither he nor Nan notice. He has no idea how lucky he is to be able to help out at the rescue centre. All those times I tried to volunteer at Hobble Farm, and they turned me down flat, and here he is complaining about getting to hang out with animals all day!

"I'm sure your mum appreciates your help," Nan

says to him. "Luna's mum worked with animals too. She was a scientist."

"That's interesting," he declares, before turning to me to ask, "What sort of science did she specialize in?"

I shrug.

"She researched animal medicine and welfare," Nan answers when I don't.

"What sort of animals? Domestic or wild?"

"Both, I think," Nan says thoughtfully. "She particularly loved dogs, but she did work with jungle animals and big cats too. She even worked with bears and wolves at one point."

Kieron's eyes widen. "Whoa! That's amazing!" He turns to address me. "And your surname is Wolf, isn't it?"

Nan looks at me expectantly.

"Yeah, it is," I mumble, folding some napkins.

"Did she get to travel to visit animals abroad?"

"A bit."

"Bet she had some great stories to report." He sighs wistfully. "When I'm a journalist, I'm going to travel all over the world. Did she ever tell you about any interesting scientific breakthroughs?"

I frown. "I … I don't remember."

"Sorry." He blushes. "I ask too many questions. Everyone always tells me that."

"I think it's nice that you ask questions," Nan insists, patting him on the hand. "It's lovely that you're so interested in other people! A sign of a good journalist, I would say."

He smiles up at her gratefully.

"Why don't you carry that salad outside and pop it on the table," she suggests.

He nods, lifting the bowl and heading out into the garden. I watch him place it down on the table before seeking out his mum.

"What a lovely boy," Nan observes.

"He talks a lot," I comment, noticing Dad laughing loudly at something Kieron says.

"Do you think so?" She raises her eyebrows. "I think he was just a bit nervous."

"He asked so many questions about Mum."

"He was making conversation."

I shrug. "Whatever."

She watches me carefully. "It's OK to be wary, Luna. This is a lot to take in, so you're allowed to take your time getting your head round the situation. But don't judge him too quickly on first impressions – it's a lot for him to navigate too."

"I'm *fine*," I tell her grumpily. "I just think he talks too much, that's all."

"All right."

We fall into silence. As I fiddle with the last few napkins, I can feel her eyes on me, but I refuse to look up at her. After a while, she sidles up to me and puts an arm around my shoulders, leaning down to kiss the top of my hair. As she holds me close, I can't help but rest my head against her, breathing in her comforting smell.

Hot tears suddenly prick at my eyes, threatening to spill over, and I blink them back.

We stand like that for a while until Nan gives me one last squeeze and then clears her throat.

"We'd better start carrying out all this food," she says. "You know how your uncle gets when he doesn't eat. Once, he was so impatient waiting for his food in a restaurant, he got thrown out the place for jumping on the table and stomping his feet! And I'm not talking about when he was a child. No, this was when he was thirty-seven years old."

I can't help but break into a smile.

"That's better." She chuckles, using her forefinger to lift my chin. "Now please could you carry the coleslaw out. And don't drop it! I only mopped these floors this morning."

On her instruction, I lift the dish and carefully carry it out to the garden.

"Luna Wolf, you're hunching!" she calls out after me.

Rolling my eyes, I pull my shoulders back, only for them to slump forwards again as soon as family members descend, attempting to drag me into their conversations. I try to avoid eye contact with all of them, staying focused on my mission of carrying the coleslaw to the table.

"Luna, over here!" Dad says, too loudly for me to pretend I haven't heard him.

I notice Kieron shift uncomfortably as Dad waves me over, and we're forced into the same vicinity yet again.

"Lucy has had the most wonderful idea," Dad says eagerly, grinning at me. "How would you like to join Kieron this summer helping out at the rescue centre?"

# CHAPTER FOUR

During that dinner, Lucy must have repeated four or five times how eager she was for me to help at the rescue centre. Which is a bit over the top, if you ask me.

"I would LOVE for you to spend some time there," she garbled. "That would be WONDERFUL, Luna. I could always do with an extra pair of hands, and your dad has told me that you love being around animals. Why don't you spend the week settling into life here in London and then, if you're still keen, you can come and help us out?"

Dad couldn't have looked happier about the idea.

"Brilliant!" he exclaimed, beaming from Lucy to

me. "That will keep you busy, right, Luna? And it will be a perfect opportunity for you to get to know each other better!"

At that point, I'd quickly made an excuse and hurried away from them. It wasn't as though I *hated* the offer. Working at a rescue centre for the summer would be amazing, and I'd love to get experience looking after the animals. But it would also mean spending time with my dad's new girlfriend.

I mostly managed to avoid her and Dad at dinner, but I kept glancing over at them every now and then, noticing little moments between them, like how they gazed at each other with dopey smiles when they thought no one was looking, and the way he put his hand on her back when he introduced her to Mum's family.

It was strange. All these months they've been seeing each other when he's come here to London, and I had no idea. I understand why Dad took his time to tell me, but I don't like the idea that he kept a secret from me. The way she was looking at him and talking about him … it's weird that someone who I didn't even know existed could be this close to my dad.

I soon got distracted by my aunts who wanted to know how I felt about the move and a new school, offering up all their recommendations for things to check out in London over the summer. I dutifully smiled and nodded as much as possible, before sliding away and escaping to my bedroom the first chance I got. I lay down on the bed and closed my eyes, enjoying the quiet for a while, until I heard them getting ready to leave and went back down to say goodbye.

As usual, it took them about an hour after they'd said they were leaving to actually go, and after we'd waved them off, Nan put her arm around my shoulders and held me tight, letting out a long, satisfied sigh.

"Being surrounded by family lifts the spirits," she declared. "Aren't we lucky?"

I nodded, because I do know that I'm very lucky to have such a big, fun family who want nothing but to see me happy. But all I feel in situations like that is awkward and self-conscious, timid and shy.

Like I'm always on the outside, looking in.

"Did you and Kieron get a chance to chat?" Dad had asked as we helped Nan clear up when the others had all left. "If you help out at the rescue centre, you'll be able to hang out with him there too."

"You don't need to force us to be friends just because you and Lucy are dating," I answered irritably.

Dad blushed, dropping his eyes. "Of course not. I wouldn't want to force anything. It's only that it might be nice." He paused, sounding tired all of a sudden. "I know that this move has come out of the blue for you, and it's not easy coming to a new place where you don't know anyone. I want you to be happy here. That's all."

I felt guilty then because he sounded so sincere.

"I know that, Dad. I'm fine. Promise," I assured him.

He didn't look convinced.

That night when I went to bed, I tried to feel positive, wondering whether I had been a bit quick to judge Kieron, and if I'd been a bit too harsh on Dad earlier when he'd been encouraging us to be friends. He was right; it would be helpful to know someone like Kieron, since I won't have much of a chance to make any other friends this summer. I won't be starting at my new school until September.

But the days following that family dinner haven't exactly been a good omen for the start of my London life. Dad has had to go into work to start his new role, so it's just been me and Nan in the house, and she is one busy lady. I had no idea she had such an active social life – there's always someone to meet or somewhere she needs to be. And when she's at home, she never sits still. She's either proudly cleaning and tidying the house, or she's preparing food for an event or for someone in the community who needs cheering up, or she's hosting friends for tea. I feel exhausted just being in her vicinity.

On Thursday, she knocks on my bedroom door and opens it to find me curled up on my bed, reading. She gives me a pointed look.

"You haven't left the house all day, Luna."

"I've been reading."

"It's not good to be all cooped up," she insists, narrowing her eyes at the pair of dirty socks I've left strewn across the carpet.

"You look nice," I say, lowering my book to admire her emerald-green dress.

"Once your dad gets home, I'm going to choir practice!" she informs me. "Would you like to join me? I'm sure they won't mind a late sign-up! The choir director actually owes me a favour – I made him a dish that he told a date last week that he'd cooked himself." She sighs. "If only his conversation had been as scintillating as my brown fish stew, then his date may have been keen for another! Still, I can ask him if you can join us too?"

"No, thanks," I say quickly. "It's not really my thing."

"You said that when I suggested you join the youth tennis club, when I found that local art club for you, when I asked you to help me with the baking for the community centre charity sale, and even when I

mentioned the events the nearby library is putting on —
and you can't tell me that reading 'isn't your thing',"
she grumbles. "I don't want you hiding away in here all
summer. London is a wonderful city to explore!"

"It's a scary city to explore."

"At first, maybe. But I told you, like everything
in life, you have to give it a chance. Don't write it off
straight away because it's different to what you know."

"Thanks, Nan, but I'm fine."

She tuts. "So you keep saying. Well, I can't force
you out the house, but have a think about trying
something new, OK?" She holds up her hands before
I can protest. "Just *think* about it."

"All right, I will," I assure her, knowing there's no
point in arguing.

She comes over and bends down to give me a kiss
on the forehead, holding my face in her hands. "You
are a special girl, Luna. Don't dim that light of yours."

With that she turns and leaves, and as she makes
her way down the stairs, I hear Dad come through the
front door, calling out that he's home. He heads into

the kitchen with Nan and they start talking in low voices, their murmurs inaudible from my room, but I can guess that I'm the topic of conversation. After a minute or so, Nan announces that she's leaving in a sing-song voice, and the front door shuts again. I go back to my reading, while Dad makes a phone call downstairs, again keeping his voice down so I can't make out who he's talking to. When he hangs up, he calls out my name and comes leaping up the stairs with boundless energy and a big smile on his face.

"Hey!" he says, coming over and ruffling my hair. "How was your day?"

"Good, how was yours?"

"Productive," he informs me, sitting down on the edge of my bed. "I'm getting used to managing the team here, but I feel a little bit like an imposter still. They're all very nice, but you never know what they're really saying behind the boss's back!"

"I'm sure they like you a lot, Dad."

"I hope so." He hesitates. "So, Nan tells me you've been doing a lot of reading lately?"

"I got some books from the library." I gesture to the stack on the bedside table.

He begins to read the titles out loud from the spines: "*The Animal Encyclopaedia*; *Amazing Animal Facts*; *Wild Species and Me* and *The Wonders of the Wolf*."

I shrug as he reads out the final one. "I thought that, because of our surname, I should at the very least know about wolves."

"Aha." He smiles, his expression softening. "Your mum would be very proud."

"Really?"

"Oh, she was fascinated by the wolf. I used to joke that my surname was the real reason she married me." He chuckles. "She promised me it wasn't, or at least not the *only* reason. Anyway, seeing these books only makes what I'm about to say even more relevant. I just got off the phone to Lucy, and I asked her whether she was still happy for you to spend time at the rescue centre. She said she was and, if you're still interested, she'd love for you to help, starting next week. You'll be paid some pocket money and everything. What do you say?"

I bite my lip, uncertain. I wouldn't hesitate in normal circumstances, but all that time at the shelter with Lucy? It would be … weird.

"You can spend as little or as much time as you like there," Dad continues, watching my expression closely. "It's only down the road, so it's easy for you to come straight home to Nan if you're not enjoying it. Why don't you do a trial run on Monday and see what you think? If you want my opinion, I think this is a great opportunity for you to get experience working with animals, like you've always wanted! And, if you need any more persuading, Lucy mentioned that one of the rescues there has had a litter of puppies recently."

He grins at me and when I don't say anything, he reaches forward and grabs my leg.

"Come on, Luna, give it a try. You'll get to spend time

with *puppies*. Don't pretend like you don't want to."

I give in, cracking a smile. "OK, I suppose I can do a trial run."

"Fantastic. I'll call Lucy and tell her the good news! She'll be thrilled."

Giving me a beaming smile, he leaps to his feet and gets his phone from his pocket as he bounds out of the room, disappearing into his bedroom and shutting the door behind him before I hear him chattering excitedly to Lucy. It's as though he radiates happiness at the mere *idea* of me and Lucy finding common ground.

Marking my page, I return the book to the top of the stack on the bedside table, before resting my head back on my pillow and closing my eyes.

I really hope I don't mess this all up for Dad.

"Remember," Nan says, putting her hands on my shoulders, "I'm only down the road. If you're absolutely miserable, you call me, and I'll stroll up to get you, OK?"

I nod, swallowing nervously.

She turns to look up at the rescue centre building. "Give it a chance," she advises, adding quietly, "and give Lucy a chance too. You know, she'll be as nervous as you are."

I snort, but Nan gives me a look.

"I'm being serious," she insists. "If anything, she's even more apprehensive than you are. She is very fond of your father, I can tell. She wants you to like her. Right" – she claps me on the back – "time to go in. Work hard and make me proud. Oh, and make sure you don't sit on any of my furniture before you've had a shower when you get back. If I see one dog hair on my embroidered cushions, Luna – ONE dog hair – you'll be in serious trouble. They were made by your cousin twice-removed who sewed them *using his toes*, I kid you not. They're one of a kind."

Lucy appears at the door of the shelter and waves at us. Nan nudges me up the pathway, watching me go in before she turns to walk home again. The reception of the rescue centre is very smart and clean, a large room with a waiting area of blue chairs to the right as you walk in and a circular reception desk in the middle. There's a man I'd guess to be in his thirties sitting behind the counter talking into the phone.

Lucy looks different to how I saw her at the family dinner — she's more relaxed and comfortable. She's wearing jeans, a black T-shirt with the rescue centre logo on it, and trainers, and has her hair tied back off her face. She offers me a warm, welcoming smile as I reach her, butterflies causing havoc in my stomach.

"Hey, Luna, I'm glad you're here. How are you today?"

"Fine, thanks," I reply shyly.

"I really appreciate you coming. I'll show you around and then you can help Kieron with a couple of jobs. Any questions, just ask, OK?"

"OK."

"Good. Let's go." She turns round and gestures to the man on the phone as we pass the reception counter to go through the double doors behind it. "That's Chris on reception."

In mid-conversation with a caller, Chris looks up at his name and smiles at me, giving me a wave, before returning his focus to the computer screen in front of him and tapping at the keyboard. I follow Lucy through the doors into a light blue corridor with several rooms leading off from it on either side.

"Down here is where the medical treatment takes place," she explains as the squeaks from my trainers on the shiny floor echo off the walls. "We only take in dogs and cats, and all of them are checked over when they arrive with us and receive any treatments and operations they may need."

She stops at a door to the right, checks through the window that it's empty, and then holds it open so I can see the room inside.

"This is one of our training rooms," she explains proudly as I peer in curiously. "We have behavioural experts who monitor each dog and run a series of tests to ensure that we spot any behavioural or attitude issues. Once we know those, we can work on them and make sure the dog ends up in the right environment when they go to their new home. Now, through here" – she shuts the door to the training room, and turns to push open a further set of double doors at the end of the corridor that opens on to a narrow outdoor pathway splitting in two directions towards separate buildings – "we have the cattery to our right, which I will show you around later, but from what I've heard about you from your dad, I have a feeling that we should go straight ahead."

Marching on, she grins at me as we reach the end of the path.

"Time to meet the dogs," she announces, holding open the door to the building, allowing me to step in first.

Big, clean kennels line either side of the room and the barking starts the moment we walk in. I can't help but break into a wide smile as the nose of an excited collie pokes through the kennel to my right, and I gaze into the loving eyes of a golden retriever to the left, both of them vying for my attention.

"Can I pet them?" I ask Lucy hopefully.

"Yes – the nervous dogs are in separate kennels and there are signs on the doors if you need to be careful or gentle with any of them. But most of these dogs will lick you to death the moment you open those kennel doors." She chuckles, reaching through the bars to give the retriever a scratch behind the ears. "Hopefully we'll find them new homes as soon as possible and they'll get a second chance to have the loving family that they deserve."

Slowly making my way down the row, it's impossible not to want to take all the dogs home with me. Along from the collie and golden retriever, there's a plucky Jack Russell that won't stop bouncing, a beagle with the waggiest tail I've ever seen, a greyhound with soul-piercing doe eyes, and a young dachshund who hasn't quite grown into her ears yet.

One of the kennels at the end has its door open and we find Kieron in there, laying out some fresh bedding for a future rescue.

"Hey, Luna," he says, offering a small smile.

"Hi."

"Kieron practically grew up here," Lucy says, looking guilty. "I'm not sure how fun he's found it, but hopefully it's all good experience!"

"I'm happy to help out," he assures her, putting a folded blanket down on the dog bed in the corner. "But I'd like it more if something happened that was worth writing about. Like a renowned politician adopting one of our dogs or something – the prime minister likes rescue dogs, doesn't he? Maybe we could write to her and ask her to consider one of ours."

Lucy laughs at him affectionately. "Kieron is always daydreaming about his next scoop."

"I have to daydream because, unfortunately, this place is dull as anything."

"That's not true," Lucy claims, jutting out her chin. "Lots of exciting things happen around here."

Kieron rolls his eyes. "You mean like last week when Chris on reception screamed and shouted about the snake in the staff room that turned out to be a dog chew rope?"

"In his defence, it did look a bit like a snake," she says. "Have you been to the cattery this morning? Did you speak to Michelle at all about little Snowflake who came in last week?"

As Lucy and Kieron launch into a conversation about Snowflake – who sounds like a lovely fluffy white cat – I'm distracted by my necklace, the pendant of which I've been nervously fiddling with while they talk. I could swear it's got weirdly warm between my fingers, and for a moment I think it might be … *flickering*. Almost as though it's glowing. It must just be catching the light in this particular room. I'm imagining things.

I tuck it into my top to stop me fidgeting any further.

While Lucy and Kieron continue to chat, I glance over my shoulder at a movement coming from the kennel behind us. Its inhabitant is a large white dog with brown splodges, floppy ears and intelligent golden eyes, who was sitting right at the back, but has stood up and seems to be staring right at me.

I tilt my head at him. He tilts his the same way.

Drifting over to his kennel, he begins to slowly make his way to the front of it, almost as though he's matching his steps to mine. I stop to look at him properly. I can't put my finger on it, but there's something about this dog. He's different. And the way he's looking at me calmly, right in the eye – it sounds strange, but I swear it's as though he *knows* me.

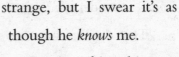

Resting his chin on the ledge, his nose pokes through the bars. I hold out my hand to him. He sniffs my skin and lets out a small, satisfied whimper. As he drops his chin, I reach through to stroke his head, and he closes his eyes.

"*Luna.*"

I turn to see Lucy and Kieron staring at me open-mouthed.

"What?" I ask, pulling my hand away from the dog. "Did I do something wrong?"

I suddenly notice the "Warning: Nervous Dog" sign pinned to the kennel bars and I flush furiously, mortified that I somehow didn't see it before.

"I'm so sorry!" I squeak, my cheeks on fire. "I didn't see the sign! I shouldn't have—"

"No, don't apologize," Lucy says hurriedly. "That was ... wonderful."

"That dog has been here almost a whole year and has refused to come near *anyone*," Kieron explains, his eyes wide with amazement. "He stays at the back of his kennel and avoids any contact with humans or other dogs. He's kept himself to himself ... until now."

I look down at the dog. He is staring up at me, as though waiting for instruction.

"Well, Luna," Lucy says, impressed, "I have a feeling you're going to fit in just fine here."

## *Seven Years Ago: After The Escape*

Athena slumps back on a red velvet wingback chair. The dog is stretched out on the rug at her feet. Letting out a long sigh, Athena smiles at the man sitting in the chair opposite her, his hands resting in his lap as he watches the dog doze contentedly.

"I'll miss him," she says, gesturing to the dog.

The man nods. "I can imagine. But he'll be safe here. They all will."

"I know."

She swallows the lump in her throat, her eyes glistening as they scan over the four other escapees, all resting in various chosen spots around the room:

an orange tabby cat curled up on a cushion, a small green gecko on the armrest of her chair, a white ferret lounging across the grand piano, and a sparrow, perched on the mantelpiece by a clock.

"How will I ever begin to thank you, Rex?" Athena asks.

Rex brushes her question off with a wave of his hand. "You don't need to thank me, Athena. I'm only glad I was able to help."

In his early sixties, Rex has thick dark hair speckled with grey, bushy eyebrows and, as ever, is sporting one of his signature colourful bow ties to brighten his crisp white shirt – today's is yellow with pink polka dots.

Athena liked Rex the moment she met him when he first interviewed her for a veterinary project she'd been working on a while ago and, despite their differences in age and background, they'd got on well from the start. Rex is a kind man, but he is also ruthless in his quest for the truth and never afraid to stand up to those who are powerful and hold them to account. Athena likes his bold questioning style and respects his insistence on extensive, thorough research. He is a brilliant investigative journalist.

When she needed to speak to someone about what she'd been tricked into by Callahan and their boss, she had known straight away that Rex was the person to go to.

It helps too, that Rex has excellent contacts and can call in a favour every now and then, such as when one is in desperate need of a getaway vehicle – a helicopter, for example. He lives in a beautiful old, secluded house in the Hertfordshire countryside, with the nearest town, Hitchin, miles away. It's the perfect place for the creatures to stay after everything they've been through. It's peaceful and quiet, and Rex adores animals. He has several rescue dogs and cats roaming about the place, not to mention the seven rescue donkeys in the paddock outside. Athena knows it's the right thing to do to leave them here, but that doesn't make it any easier.

"I will keep you updated on them," Rex promises,

as though reading her mind. "And you know that you're always welcome to visit."

"I'm not sure that is a good idea. I can't risk Callahan following me here once he's tracked me down."

Rex furrows his eyebrows in concern. "Are you sure you'll be safe?"

She nods. "Yes."

"How can you be so sure?"

She reaches into her pocket and pulls out a small, jagged blue stone, the only remaining piece of the stolen magical source. Athena had cut it off before they'd blown the rest of it to smithereens in the middle of Rex's lawn.

"I'm the only person who's ever been able to get this to work," she says, holding the stone up so it glints in the light. "They wouldn't risk harming me in case they might need me again in the future."

"But we'll never let them get that far, right?"

"Thanks to your video, they think the magic is destroyed." She nods. "And with the animals safely hidden away here, they have no way of moving forward with the project. Maybe they'll try to find other ways or try to find more of the magical source somehow, but that won't be for a very long time."

"We need to expose them," Rex says firmly. "Once everyone reads about what they've tried to do—"

"I think they'll have destroyed every last bit of evidence by now," Athena says glumly, returning the pendant to her pocket. "You'll have trouble proving anything without showing everyone the animals – and we don't want that. No one can ever know they're here."

"I'll write the piece exposing them anyway, and maybe one day it will be published or will come in useful," he says, frowning. "I have to *try*."

She smiles at his determination. "I know. But even if no one reads your piece, please remember just how much you've done for me and these animals. You've given them a shot at a good life. That is so much more important."

Glancing around the room, she suddenly starts,

pointing at the door and gasping, "Donkey!"

Rex spins in his chair to see that one of the donkeys has come wandering into the room and is attempting to munch the flowers arranged in a vase on top of the grand piano.

"Oh, for goodness' sake, they're always getting into the house," he sighs, pushing himself to his feet as Athena follows suit, laughing heartily. "I leave one door open, and they let themselves in quite happily as though they own the place!"

Once she's helped Rex turn the donkey around and led it back out of the house, she gives Rex a hug goodbye.

"You get home to your little girl," he says warmly, before hesitating. "Do your family know about this?"

She shakes her head. "You know how secret it was – I wasn't allowed to tell them anything. And anyway, it's better they don't know about it for their own safety."

He nods in agreement. "Well, you head off and get some rest. And don't worry about a thing. I know how special these animals are, and trust me, there's no better place for them. They'll be very happy here, I promise."

"Thanks, Rex."

She looks down at the animals who have all loyally followed her outside.

"I'm not very good at goodbyes," she admits, her voice breaking slightly.

She bends to stroke the cat, who is rubbing against her calves. The ferret runs up her leg and into her arms, and she holds out a hand for the gecko to hop up on to. The sparrow comes to land on her shoulder.

"Stay safe, all right?" Athena instructs them all, before passing the ferret and gecko over to Rex.

She turns her attention to the dog, crouching down to be at his level.

He leans forward to rest his forehead against hers. They stay like that in silence for a moment. She doesn't need to explain anything to him. He already knows.

Forcing herself to break apart from him and stand up straight, she thanks Rex one final time, before turning to leave. As she reaches her car – parked in the driveway – she realizes the sparrow is still perched on her shoulder.

"Off you go," she says, stroking the sparrow's feathers with her knuckle.

There's a sudden blinding flash of blue light and, launching herself off Athena's shoulder, the sparrow transforms into a magnificent eagle. Rex gasps in amazement.

Athena smiles to herself.

"You're free now," she whispers, watching the eagle soar through the air.

She climbs into her car, turns the key in the ignition and begins the drive home to her family.

# CHAPTER FIVE

It has taken a week, but I've fallen into a routine at the rescue centre.

When I wake up in the mornings, I throw on one of the black T-shirts Lucy gave me and run downstairs for a quick breakfast before making my way to the shelter, usually with a stern warning from Nan to stand up straight, stop bringing home dog hairs on my clothes, and to make sure I eat a good lunch or else I might faint like my great, great-aunt Kendall did that time at an elegant tea party thrown for an ambassador, face-planting a perfectly good lemon tart and ruining it for everyone else.

Kieron and I are allowed to attend the morning meeting during which Lucy tells the team about any new additions to the centre and runs through any necessary admin, before the two of us head to the "dog kitchen" to help measure out each dog's breakfast and prepare it in their individual bowls. This is one of my

favourite parts of the day because, as soon as the dogs hear us coming through the doors with their bowls clanging together, they get overexcited, jumping for joy, spinning around in circles and greeting us with happy barks and impatient whines.

We try our best to get each one to sit before they get their meal, a trick that their future owners will hopefully appreciate, and then place it down for them to gobble up in a matter of seconds. Sometimes there will be a slightly more nervous dog who will wait for us to leave the kennel before they start eating, but as the days go on, it's amazing to see apprehensive dogs starting to come out of their shells and learn to trust us.

Lucy has told me that it's all about patience – we don't know the backstory of some of the dogs, or we know they've had a tough start to life, so we need to slowly and gently guide them in their adjustment to their new surroundings and help them to understand that they're safe here with us. In fact, Lucy said, as the team are always so busy, one of the most helpful things that Kieron and I can do is to take the time to sit with those nervous dogs in their kennels and let them approach us when they're ready. Sometimes it can take an hour or so, and other times they don't approach at all, but that's OK, we're still getting them used to human company in a calm manner, and gradually they'll build up the courage.

That's why it was so strange, Lucy said, that the large white dog with brown splodges had come right up to me on my first day. He hadn't approached anyone before, not even Lucy, who had put in the effort to sit in his kennel for hours at weekends.

"Then you walked in and straight away he trusted you," she said, shaking her head in disbelief. "That really was the most bizarre and wonderful moment. But, as I've said a thousand times, dogs can sense things us humans can't. And that dog could sense something about you, Luna."

I don't know if she's saying these things to make me feel better about myself, but it's hard not to feel proud about it. It's nice to feel chosen, especially for me; I've never felt special before. But I feel important to this dog.

His name is Silver. Kieron named him when he arrived at the shelter and claims he picked the name because he wanted something a bit grand, as the dog is so big, and one evening, Kieron took him outside on his lead for his night-time toilet trip and apparently he howled at the full moon, which Kieron poetically describes as looking like a giant silver pendant in the sky.

I haven't admitted as much to Kieron, but I think it's the perfect name. He looks like a Silver.

Silver is the shelter's longest-visiting resident by a long way. He's been here almost a year, and no one has reserved him or fallen in love with him when they've come round to look at the dogs. Lucy explained that it's because Silver would hide away when anyone strolled down looking into the kennels, and if anyone looked remotely interested, Silver would bare his teeth at them before ducking his head down again, as though he was telling them not to get any ideas.

"Do you know what's even stranger about Silver taking a liking to you?" Lucy said during my first few days. "He was found on your nan's doorstep. She opened the door one morning and there he was, standing right outside looking at her."

"I think I remember her mentioning him. She said he didn't want to move," I recalled.

"That's right." She nodded. "Luckily, I had one of the team with me so we could get the lead on him, but it took us a long time. Even when we got the lead around his neck, he refused to budge. He was so stubborn! It was as though he'd decided to stay at your nan's house."

"She'd never allow that. He picked the wrong house."

"I'm not so sure," Lucy said, watching me curiously. "Maybe he knew all along that it was the right one."

While helping where I'm needed, I've spent a lot of time getting to know Silver. Lucy encouraged it, since I am the only one who has managed to earn his trust, I've been allowed to sit in his kennel on my breaks and take him for walks. I've had no trouble at all with him. Since our first meeting, he's come right up to me and let me sit next to him, stroking his head and putting the lead on him to go for a stroll. He happily trots alongside me, glancing up at me constantly to check I'm all right. I've taken him out into the garden and played fetch with him, which he absolutely loves – now when I come to his kennel holding the ball, his eyes brighten and he bounds over, desperate to jump up at me, which always makes me laugh because he's so big that his paws reach my shoulders.

One of the reasons I like spending time with Silver is it gives me an excuse not to hang around too much with Kieron or Lucy. I know that sounds mean, but I'm still not entirely comfortable around them.

At least with Lucy we can talk about the rescue centre, and she can give me instructions or teach me something about the dogs, so we don't have to have any uncomfortable general conversation. But with Kieron I feel particularly awkward. We don't have much in common – he's only working at the centre because of his mum, not because he really wants to be here – and any time we do talk, his observations seem to irritate me.

Like when we're getting the food ready for a litter of puppies and, when I hear they've already all been reserved, I mention that it makes me feel a bit sad that the puppies have already been snapped up, whereas older dogs, like Silver, haven't found a home yet.

"You can't fool me," Kieron says while we measure the puppies' kibble into tiny little bowls. "If anyone came to the centre to take Silver home, you'd be devastated."

"That's not true!"

Kieron gives me a look. "Oh, really? So, you wouldn't mind if someone strolled in today, saw Silver, decided to adopt him, and you'd never see him again."

Just the thought of it makes me want to burst into tears.

"I understand that it's more important for Silver to find a happy home than for me to get to spend time with him," I insist.

"Sure," Kieron mutters under his breath.

*You see?* He acts as though he knows me when he doesn't know me at all! And now the idea of Silver leaving has put me in a terrible mood. I clang the bowls as I move them about a bit too roughly.

Maybe he notices that he's annoyed me because, after glancing in my direction, Kieron clears his throat and says, "Mum has always said that's the hardest part of the job. You build a relationship with the animals here and then you have to say goodbye. Even though you know it's best for them, it doesn't make it any easier."

I press my lips together, acknowledging the truth of that statement.

"I wasn't implying that you didn't want the best for Silver," he adds tiredly. "I was just … look, I think it's cool that you have a connection with him."

I nod, feeling a little guilty. I don't mean to give him a hard time. I'm still a bit prickly with him because of the strange situation Dad threw me into, and I know that none of that is Kieron's fault.

I'm about to apologize for being so sensitive when Lucy comes bustling into the room, reading something on her phone.

"Ah, there you two are. Are you feeding the puppies?"

Kieron gestures to the bowls. "We have it all under control."

"And you've marked it on the chart?"

"I was just about to," Kieron says hurriedly, grabbing a pen. He's been told off before for forgetting to make a note that they've been fed – on occasion, they've had more than one breakfast.

"Well done." She grins at him, before turning

her attention to me. "Luna, I've been thinking — how would you feel about sitting in on a training session with one of our behaviour experts tomorrow? Silver refuses to take any notice of her, so I thought it might be a good idea for you to learn a few tips from her. Then you could have a go at giving Silver some training lessons and we can see how we get on. None of us have been able to get him to do anything before, but you might have better luck, especially as he's responding to you so well on the lead already."

"I would love to!" I say excitedly. "Thank you!"

"Great."

"I hope you get to use a tennis-ball blaster," Kieron says, his eyes brightening. "They're so cool, like water guns, but they shoot out tennis balls. They go so far!"

"I think she'll start with the basics first." Lucy laughs. "But once Silver has got good recall and practised his fetch skills, then I'm sure you can have a go with the tennis-ball blaster. Kieron, why don't you bring your camera in tomorrow?" She reaches over to ruffle his hair as she tells me, "I got him a fancy professional camera for Christmas. My budding journalist."

He frowns at her, swatting away her hand. "Why would you want me to bring it in?"

"To take some photos of Silver training with Luna. Maybe that will help his online profile and get a future owner interested in him."

My heart sinks. Kieron glances at me.

"Sure," he says quietly. "Good idea."

"That's all sorted then," Lucy declares, before holding the door open for us. "Off you go. Back to work."

A few days later, I'm heading out of the shelter after saying goodnight to Silver – a long drawn-out process that involves me sitting on the floor while he rests his head in my lap until I'm told that the building is being locked up – when something catches my eye on the noticeboard that hangs on the wall in reception. It's a pinboard with pictures of old canine residents, staff members at work, cut-out newspaper articles about the shelter, and thank-you letters from owners giving updates on how their rescues are settling in at their new homes.

But there's a brand-new picture right in the middle of the board: it's one of the photos that Kieron took the other day of me and Silver. I'm looking at the camera with a wide grin across my face and my arm around Silver, who happens to also have been looking right at the lens in that moment with his tongue hanging out so it looks like he's smiling for the photo.

I stop in my tracks to stare up at it.

"What do you think?" Lucy asks, coming over to stand next to me.

"I love that picture. How come it's up on the wall, though? That's only for team members."

"Exactly. You're one of the team now, Luna."

"I am?"

"Definitely. Thank you so much for all your work. You should be off having fun during your summer holidays, and yet you're here every day. I really appreciate it."

I drop my eyes to the ground, admitting, "I like it here."

"I'm glad."

We fall into silence for a bit, until she eventually speaks.

"You know, I've always felt more at home around animals. If you don't mind me saying it, I think you're a bit like that too. I can see that you come alive when you're around them. So, I want you to know that if you ever feel … down or confused or overwhelmed … well, you're always welcome to come here and spend time with the dogs. They seem to make everything that bit better when I feel that way anyway. And" – she pauses – "I'm always here too if you want to talk. As a friend."

I glance up at her. She's not looking at me, instead her eyes are fixed straight ahead on the noticeboard, and I see that she's fidgeting with the bottom material of her T-shirt. I think about my first day here when Nan said that Lucy would be nervous about the new situation too, despite how confident and cool she may seem.

Even though we see each other almost every day at the rescue centre, we haven't spent much time together outside of it, and I know that's because Dad doesn't want to rush me into anything. Apart from that family dinner where we did our introductions, he hasn't really spent much time with Lucy, insisting he wants us to find our feet here first – I know that really he means me, though.

He's found his feet just fine. It's me that's been all wobbly.

"Thank you," I say. "That's really nice of you."

"No problem."

I hesitate. "Lucy?"

"Mm?"

"Would you and Kieron like to come over for lunch with me, Dad and Nan this weekend?"

She turns to look at me in surprise, before a smile breaks across her face. "I'd love that! Thank you, Luna."

We fall into silence again, but something seems to

have lifted in the air, the two of us that little bit more comfortable next to each other.

"That really is a lovely picture," Lucy says, nodding to the one of me and Silver. "You look very happy."

She's correct, I realize, gazing up at it.

Next to Silver, I look right at home.

# CHAPTER SIX

Dad is very flustered.

Nan and I are finding his antics in the kitchen extremely entertaining. Nan is sitting with a cup of tea, sipping contentedly, as Dad flies around the place, checking the temperature of the oven over and over again, yelping as he suddenly remembers something he's forgotten to get out of the fridge, and rearranging the pots and the pans on the hobs.

He insisted on doing all the cooking for today and decided on a traditional English Sunday roast dinner of Yorkshire puddings, potatoes, cabbage, honey carrots and parsnips, and a ginormous harissa-roasted

cauliflower. Nan offered to help, but he's been very firm that he wants to do it all himself, so the two of us are relegated to setting the table and watching his hair get slowly more and more dishevelled as he continues to run his hands through it in a state of panic, while at the same time insisting he has everything under control.

He's been excited about today ever since I mentioned I'd invited Lucy and Kieron over for a meal. I told him and Nan over dinner, and he was so startled by my revelation that he dropped his fork and it clattered loudly on to his plate, making Nan and I jump. He tried to play it cool, but I could tell I'd made his day.

As Dad bustles about, getting everything ready and speaking out loud to himself about what he needs to do next, the doorbell goes. Nan sends me to answer it so she can continue to watch Dad in amusement while enjoying her tea.

"Sorry we're a bit late," Lucy says as I stand back to let them in. "Kieron was playing on his computer with his headphones on and forgot the time."

"I wasn't *playing* on my computer," Kieron huffs, irritated at the assumption. "I was researching the recent string of break-ins at rescue centres and trying to establish a pattern so that I can help to catch the culprits. It's called *investigating*."

"Wait, what? Rescue centres are being broken into?" I check, horrified.

"None of the animals were taken, don't worry,"

Lucy says, holding up her hands. "And there haven't been any in this area. If you want my opinion, it's pranksters."

"We should up the security on the shelter, just in case," Kieron insists.

"I agree," I say, nodding vigorously. "We don't want to take any chances."

"We already have CCTV and an alarm. You see, Kieron?" Lucy sighs. "I told you not to tell Luna about this; she's just going to worry now. I promise you, Luna, our animals are safe and sound."

She wanders through into the kitchen and receives a greeting from Nan and a very frazzled Dad. Remaining in the hallway, I turn back to Kieron.

"Why would there be break-ins but no animals taken?" I ask, intrigued.

"You want my theory? I think they are looking for something," Kieron reveals conspiratorially. "I did some digging and in each case the intruders were in and out in a matter of minutes. I tried to call the centres to get some more information, but as soon as

I told them I was a reporter, they told me the police investigation was still ongoing and they couldn't comment."

"What would burglars be looking for at a rescue centre?"

"Maybe one of them lost their dog."

"Why would you need to break-in for that? You'd just go and check if they were there."

"Yeah, it's very strange. That's why I was looking into it."

"Luna! Kieron! Come through here, please, food is about to be served," Nan calls out, and we scurry through to the kitchen.

It's hard to concentrate on the meal when I'm so distracted by these rescue centre break-ins. I'm sure it's nothing to worry about and, as Lucy said, if they didn't take anything, then maybe it is just someone playing a horrible prank. I hope that whatever it is, it stops and our shelter isn't targeted.

"This is *delicious*," Lucy enthuses after the first mouthful of cauliflower, causing Dad's tense shoulders that are up around his ears to finally relax with relief.

"Richard, it's excellent," Nan confirms proudly.

"It must have taken you a long time to prepare all this," Lucy says.

"Oh, not really," Dad says breezily with a wave of his hand as Nan and I share a secretive smile across the table. "There's plenty more for seconds too."

"I had no idea you were such a good cook," Lucy admits, digging into the roast potatoes.

"I'm nothing compared to Clementine," he says, nodding to Nan who shakes her head modestly. "But I enjoy cooking when I get the chance, which isn't very often."

"You can't get much opportunity either, what with running the shelter," Nan observes to Lucy. "You must be run off your feet there."

"It's been a lot easier having these two around to help out this summer," she replies, looking at me and Kieron. "Has Luna told you about Silver?"

"Has she? HA!" Nan sighs. "We know all about

118

Silver. We hear about Silver's progress every single day without fail."

"Their connection is undeniable," Lucy says, taking a sip of her drink. "I've never seen a dog respond to a human like that before. He singled her out. It's like he *chose* her."

"I hope you're not implying that she should take that dog home," Nan says, giving her a stern look. "If I've said it once, I'll say it again. A dog may well be a friendly creature, but they are also a nuisance, and I won't have one lounging on my sofa acting like it owns the place. Next thing you know it will be in my bed, wearing my nightie, nestled under my duvet. I've seen it before. People treat them like humans! Fur everywhere."

"Nan!" I sigh. "That's not always the case."

"Yes, it is," she claims stubbornly. "Mr Gregory from down the road got that puppy last year, and he went on and on about how it was a timid little thing, so sweet, so gentle. What happened next? The puppy grew up to be as big as a horse. Pulled him right off his feet running across the park on his lead after a squirrel. Mr Gregory had to get three stitches."

"I don't believe that story," I say. "It sounds made up."

"Oh, really?" She raises her eyebrows at me. "I suppose you don't believe me when I tell you that when I last visited him, I spent two seconds on Mr Gregory's sofa – TWO seconds – and I had so many dog hairs clinging to my trousers when I left that I had to throw them away. Nothing could be done to save them."

"Nan! That's obviously not true!"

"It is true! Dogs cannot be controlled in the home. One look from a Great Dane at your furnishings and they're ruined."

"Silver wouldn't ruin any furnishings," I inform her stubbornly.

"How would you know?"

"Because I *know* him. And what does it matter if dogs do cause a little mess? Isn't it worth that for the companionship?"

"You can get companionship from a human,"

Nan argues.

"It's not the same."

"Oh?"

"It's *not*," I tell her. "If you gave a dog a chance, you would see that. I bet if I brought Silver home, you would fall in love with him right away, and he would love you back. Dogs do that, you know – they love you, no matter what. They don't care who you are or whether you're cool or popular or clever. If you love them, they love you. Why wouldn't you want an animal like that by your side?"

"I would like an animal like that by my side *if* they came with a vacuum cleaner that cleaned up after them wherever they went and an inbuilt air freshener in their tail to do a quick spritz as they leave a room."

"You've written off all dogs when you've never even had one!"

"You don't know the hard work that goes into keeping a house clean!"

I open my mouth to argue back when I notice Dad lifting his napkin and dabbing at his eyes. Nan is

121

similarly taken aback by his reaction.

"What's wrong, Richard? Luna and I were only having a discussion, there's no need to get upset."

"Sorry, Dad," I say quickly, my face growing hot with embarrassment as I realize I may have got a bit carried away arguing with Nan in front of Lucy and Kieron.

Dad shakes his head and sniffs, breaking into a smile. "No, no, it's not that. I'm sorry, I just … well, you two arguing like that over having a dog and Luna wearing that necklace… It reminded me a lot of how you used to debate the exact same topic with Athena. Sorry, I didn't mean to get emotional. Sometimes, Luna, you remind me so much of your mother."

Nan's face softens. "You know, I thought I'd had this conversation once or twice before. A strange bout of déjà vu."

Lucy reaches over to take Dad's hand in hers, giving it a comforting squeeze.

"Did Athena ever win the argument?" Kieron wants to know.

"Of course not," Nan says, the corners of her

mouth twitching into a smile. "And neither will Luna, thank you very much."

"Oh, I wouldn't be so sure," Lucy says, grinning. "The past couple of weeks have proven to me that Luna can be very motivated and determined when she wants to be, and there's still time yet for her to win you over. Not to mention Silver really is a very sweet dog who would look particularly handsome sitting on your sofa, Clementine."

"And he'd look even better wearing her nightie," Kieron adds mischievously.

Everyone bursts out laughing. Except Nan, that is.

"Luna, come with me for a moment," Nan says, catching me as I emerge from the bathroom after brushing my teeth that night. She ushers me into her bedroom. "I've been meaning to give you these since you moved in, but I kept forgetting. Can you look under the bed for me – there should be a box there."

Getting on to my hands and knees, I peer under her bed and drag out a brown box that looks as though it's filled with old files and stacks of paper.

"There you go," she says proudly as though I should understand what all of this is straight away.

"What is it?" I ask, picking up the top piece of paper that has a load of scribbled notes and equations dotted around it.

"These are some of your mother's things," she informs me, sitting on the bed near to where I'm kneeling so she can look over my shoulder. "She kept it all here, stuffed in her desk and when you and Richard decided to move in, I thought I'd clear out the furniture in her room so you could use the drawers of the desk if you needed. I think it must be things from her old office that was fairly near here. Anyway, our discussion tonight about the dogs reminded me I'd been meaning to show it to you. There are some old photos in there and some of her science papers. You and Richard should go through them and see if you'd like to keep any of it."

"Wow, Nan. Thanks."

"It could all be rubbish," she muses. "But you

never know. You might find a gem in there. The photo framed by your bed? I found that among these things."

I start to rifle through the papers extremely carefully, worried that I'll smudge or tear something that could be meaningful. Most of it does seem to be her workings-out, which will be amazing to hold on to, and I only wish that I could decipher any of it, but science and maths have never been my strong suit.

There are several files with "TOP SECRET" stamped across the front and a strange symbol just below that I don't recognize – the letter "M" placed in the middle of a set of ferocious jaws.

"What does this symbol mean?" I ask Nan, pointing at it, but she shrugs.

"I have no idea.
I assumed it was a
company logo of
some kind."

The files are all
empty, which is a

shame because the TOP SECRET written on them got me all excited, as though I was about to find something of national importance.

"I wonder what was in these," I say, unable to hide the disappointment in my voice as I put them down.

"Oh, she was always working on 'secretive' projects," Nan says with a dismissive wave of her hand. "But they were only secretive because the company she was working for didn't want rival companies to get hold of her research. The information in those files would have meant nothing to us, I'm sure."

Underneath the files, slipped between two pages of scribbled notes, is a photo.

As I pull it out to examine it, I realize that it's not the whole picture – someone has ripped one end of it away. It's a photo of Mum in her lab coat, standing next to another scientist, a man with blonde curly hair, a bushy moustache and glasses. I don't recognize him. And then I can just make out the arm of someone else who was standing next to him, but that's where the picture has been torn. All you can make out of the final figure in the picture is that he wasn't in a lab coat, but it looks like he's wearing a suit, and he has a chunky, expensive-looking gold watch on his wrist.

"Do you know who this is?" I ask Nan, holding up the picture so she can see.

She shakes her head. "No. Must have been an old colleague."

I put the photo back into the box and return the empty files too.

"Thanks so much for this, Nan. I'll go through it properly."

"You're welcome," she says, leaning down to stroke my cheek before getting up and going over to her dressing table. "You go and get a good night's sleep."

Lifting the box, I get to my feet and carry it out, before stopping in her doorway.

"Nan?" I begin.

"Yes?"

"When you and Mum argued about having a dog,

did she ever say anything that made you close to caving in and letting her have her way?"

Nan raises her eyebrows at me. "You asking for tips on how to beat me?"

"Worth a try."

She laughs. "I respect your candour. If you must know, there was one point she made that made me think twice."

"What was it?"

"She said that when you have a dog at your side, you're never truly alone." She tilts her head at me. "Not too dissimilar to the arguments you were making tonight."

"And that made you think twice?"

"It can get lonely in this house sometimes. That's why I'm so grateful to have you and your dad here for the moment, and why I enjoy family get-togethers so much. Now it's getting late. Off you go to bed."

I nod, unable to stop a smile.

"Why are you smiling so smugly all of a sudden?" she says, putting her hands on her hips.

"Because before I thought there was no hope of having Silver here, but now I think there might be," I admit, turning away with my box. "I won't give up yet."

"Now, wait just a second—"

"Night, Nan!" I call out over my shoulder, heading towards my room and shutting the door before she can argue back.

# ✳ CHAPTER SEVEN

"Hi, Luna!" Dad says, wandering down the row of kennels in the rescue centre and setting off all the dogs in a chorus of excitable barking.

I look up in surprise from putting down a fresh bowl of water in the kennel of a snooty chihuahua, who rarely deigns to get up from her bed and looks at me in a way that makes me feel like her inferior.

"Dad! What are you doing here?"

"I got home from work early today and thought I'd come see you in your element. That OK?"

"Yeah." I smile, coming out of the chihuahua's kennel and shutting the door behind me. "This is

Tallulah. She thinks I'm her personal butler."

"Ah." He peers at her through the bars. She narrows her eyes at him. "I don't think she's very impressed with me."

"She's not very impressed with anyone. Her new owner is coming to pick her up tomorrow — she is also the kind of lady who doesn't seem impressed with anyone, so I think they're perfect for one another. She asked me why Tallulah was wearing a dark collar when it was obvious she'd be better suited to a pastel colour and didn't seem to care when I explained that all the rescue collars are the same. She said she's bought Tallulah a pink designer diamanté collar that will match her pink designer bed. It's safe to say that Tallulah is going to have a very happy life in her new Islington home."

Dad bursts out laughing as Tallulah rests her head down on her blanket, closes her eyes and lets out a long sigh, as though dismissing us from her vicinity.

"Can I meet the famous Silver?" he asks.

"This way," I say, leading him down to the end

kennel. "I was going to take him out for some training in the garden if you want to join?"

"Sounds like a great plan."

Silver is waiting for me as usual when we reach his kennel, sitting bolt upright by the door, his eyes fixed on me as we approach.

"He is very handsome," Dad remarks, stopping next to me and putting his hands on his hips. "He also looks vaguely familiar ... where have I seen him before?"

"The photo on the pinboard as you walk in the centre?" I suggest. "Kieron took it."

"No, that's not it." He frowns. "I've seen this dog before, a long time ago."

"Oh, I know," I say, remembering something I'd also thought when I first met Silver. "The photo in my room at Nan's of Mum. The dog in that one looks a bit like Silver."

"That's right," Dad says slowly, his eyes widening in amazement. "I remember that dog. Athena used to talk about him a lot and show me pictures of him. They look so similar."

"Bet he wasn't as beautiful as my Silver," I say, opening the kennel door. He stalks out and sits at my side, looking Dad up and down. "Silver, I'd like you to meet my dad. Dad, this is Silver."

"A pleasure to make your acquaintance, Silver," Dad says, reaching out to let Silver sniff his hand, before stroking his head. Silver gives him a gentle lick on the wrist. "He's lovely."

"I know, right? Wait until you see all his new tricks! Come on, let's go," I say, putting Silver's lead on and taking him outside to the garden, Dad following behind.

Since I've been trying out some training with Silver, I've realized that, as I suspected, he is fiercely intelligent and a fast learner, so I'm excited to show off his progress to Dad and even more pleased when Lucy appears at the garden gate, coming in to join us.

"How was your day, Richard?" she asks, greeting him with a big smile as I ask Silver to sit neatly next to me and wait.

"Not too busy, so I got off early and came straight

here. I thought it would be fun to see what Luna has been getting up to. Is Kieron around?"

"He went home around lunchtime," she tells him as I absent-mindedly stroke Silver's soft ears and he leans his head against my leg. "He's gone to a birthday party this afternoon."

"Oh, that's nice," Dad says. "Is it one of his friends from school?"

She pauses, answering quietly, "Actually, I don't think Kieron and this boy get on that well. I think his parents made him invite the whole class. Kieron was very nervous about going, so I'm going to go pick him up soon."

I don't say anything, but I know exactly how Kieron feels. I once went to someone's party, but never would have got the invite if her dad hadn't insisted she ask everyone in our year group to come. It was in her garden, and I stood at the side the entire time feeling awkward. No one talked to me.

"Luna was about to show me some of Silver's new tricks," Dad tells Lucy. "I take it you've already seen what he can do?"

"Actually, I haven't yet," she says, folding her arms. "How are you getting on with it, Luna?"

"Really well. I think you're going to be pleased with him," I say confidently.

"All right then," Lucy says, sharing a smile with Dad. "Go ahead."

"We haven't done this in front of an audience before, though, so keep that in mind," I add quickly. Silver doesn't seem fazed by either of them being there and, as ever, has his eyes fixed on me, but still – I don't want to raise their expectations too much.

I start with the basic training, telling Silver to heel as I take off his lead and walk him around the garden. He stays right by my side the whole way around and, at my command, sits beautifully when we get back to them again.

"Brilliant," Lucy comments, looking impressed.

"We're only just getting started," I inform her proudly.

Turning to face Silver, I ask him for "paw" and then "other paw"; he lies down, then rolls over when

I ask; when I tap my shoulder and say "up", he jumps up, resting his paws on my shoulders, before sitting down again when I tell him to; I ask him to "speak" and he barks once; and then I reach into my pocket for a ball and throw it to the end of the garden, telling him to wait – he doesn't move a muscle until I tell him to "fetch", returning it perfectly into my hands. As I conclude the demonstration by asking him to sit again, I look to see Lucy and Dad's reactions.

Both of them are standing side by side with their mouths hanging open.

"Luna," Lucy says, looking at us in disbelief, "you've done all that in a *week*?"

"It's all Silver," I insist, giving him a pat on the head. "It's as though he can read my mind and knows what I'm asking him to do before I say anything."

"It's like you're connected somehow," Dad croaks, so shocked he can barely get his words out. "The way he looks at you…"

"I know!" Lucy nods in agreement, without him needing to finish his sentence. "It's weird, isn't it?

I told you! He won't respond to anyone else. He'll barely *look* at anyone else."

Dad exhales, shaking his head. "That really is quite something."

"If you want my opinion, Richard, and I hope I'm not overstepping the mark here," Lucy says, "but Silver belongs with Luna."

My heart swells at her words, and I look down affectionately at Silver, who gazes back at me with his bright, devoted eyes.

"I would have to agree," Dad says, running a hand through his hair. "He does seem to have really taken to you, Luna. And something's changed about you too."

"Me?" I ask in surprise.

"Yes. Ever since you met that dog, it's like you've become … more yourself. As though the light in you is shining that bit brighter. He's brought you out of your shell."

"It sounds like you have the same wonderful affinity to dogs as your mother did, from what I've heard about her," Lucy comments gently.

Flattered, my hand automatically flies to my necklace, and I twist the pendant around in my fingers. "I hope so," I say quietly.

Lucy and Dad share a look. She seems to be encouraging him to say something – it takes him a moment, but then he breaks into a smile and nods, as though giving in.

She claps her hands excitedly. "Luna, your dad and I have something to discuss with you. We've been talking and I made a suggestion that I *think* he has just this moment agreed to. Richard?"

"Yes," he says at her prompt. "Lucy has been honest about her opinion that you and Silver have a special bond, and it doesn't seem right for Silver to end up with another family. And, from what I've just seen, I would agree."

"Not that anyone has shown any interest in Silver, anyway," Lucy jumps in. "It's fate that he was meant to stay at the rescue centre this long until you arrived, Luna."

"I know that Nan won't have dogs in her house,

but we won't be living with her for ever," Dad continues to me. "In fact, now that I'm getting into my new routine at work and everything is going well, I think it's about time you and I start looking for our own place. Hopefully, we'll be able to find a house nearby."

"So, I propose that Silver stays here at the rescue centre until you've got your new home ready, *but* he will no longer be available for adoption," Lucy emphasizes.

"And that's because, as of today, if you would like, Silver will officially be your dog, Luna," Dad concludes. "What do you think?"

I stare at him, hardly daring to believe what he's saying.

My dog. Silver would be *my dog*.

THIS IS THE BEST DAY OF MY LIFE!

Elated, I squeal with joy and rush into Dad's open arms, almost winding him.

"DAD! Thank you, thank you, thank you!" I cry, feeling so happy I think I might burst. "I would love that so much!"

"Don't thank me…" Dad laughs as I pull away. "It was all Lucy's idea."

"Thank you, Lucy," I say, beaming at her.

"To be honest, I'm not sure this wasn't all Silver's idea," she corrects, looking over at him with a sly smile. "Anyone would think he's been waiting for you all this time."

Rushing back to Silver, I kneel down next to him and throw my arms around his neck. He nuzzles into me, licking my ear as I hold him tight and blink back tears of happiness. Dad puts his arm around Lucy, and I pretend not to see as he gives her a kiss on the cheek. The doorbell of the shelter suddenly echoes through the building, causing Lucy to look confused.

"That's strange. We're closed," she remarks. "I put up the sign."

"Maybe Chris forgot his keys," I say, unable to wipe the smile off my face as I give Silver a good neck scratch.

"I'll go check it out," she says.

"I'll come with you," Dad offers.

"Are you OK to put Silver back in his kennel?" Lucy asks me, already knowing the answer. "Then come meet us in reception and I'll lock up for the night."

"All right, see you in a bit," I say.

They head back inside, while Silver and I celebrate by running up and down the garden a couple of times, Silver bouncing along beside me, seemingly picking up on my happy mood by leaping for joy and yapping happily. By the time I head back to the kennels, I'm out of breath, laughing and wheezing, with Silver trotting contentedly next to me. It's rescue centre rules to put the dogs on the lead as soon as we exit the secured garden, so I dutifully do so even though, as I say to Silver, I know he'd never leave my side.

When we head inside, I'm about to put Silver back in his kennel when I hear raised voices coming from reception. Distracted, I continue past the kennels with Silver still beside me, towards the main building. I open the door a fraction so I can peer down the corridor.

Lucy seems to be trying to calm down a man standing just outside the front door, demanding to be allowed in. I can't see what he looks like because Lucy is blocking him and Dad is standing behind her for support.

"It will only take a minute," the man is grumbling. "I'm looking for a very specific type of dog. I want to see the dogs available for adoption."

"Sorry, sir, but as I've said, the shelter is closed, no exceptions," Lucy explains, keeping her cool in the face of his anger. "We don't allow walk-ins anyway, I'm afraid. You have to make an appointment. It's the same for all potential owners. We need to make sure that our dogs are going to the right type of homes and that you're prepared for the responsibilities. Getting to know you beforehand helps us to match you to a suitable dog."

"I don't need to be matched! I know what I want!"

"You can tell us your preferences when you make an appointment," Lucy says, completely unfazed by his rude and abrupt demeanour.

"It will take just a few minutes for me to look around your kennels," the man insists.

Silver lets out a low and threatening growl. I look down at him, and he's stood in a position that looks as though he's ready to pounce, his head low to the ground, his eyes focused on where they're standing.

I pull him back and shut the door, placing a comforting hand on the fur of his back. As I do so, I feel a surge of warmth flood through my body and there's a sudden flash of blinding blue light.

When it fades, I gasp in horror, stumbling backwards.

Where Silver was standing is now a giant *wolf*.

# CHAPTER EIGHT

Baring its teeth, the wolf growls at the shut door.

Backed up against the wall, I'm frozen in shock. The wolf turns its head to look at me and stops growling, fixing his familiar golden eyes on mine. The red lead that was around my dog's neck hangs limply from the wolf's.

"S-Silver?" I whisper, staring at him in disbelief.

He gives me a slight bow of his head and my fear disappears. Any worry or shock fizzles in an instant, and I'm completely comforted in the company of this incredible animal. He seems to understand that I'm not scared of him, padding towards me so that when

I reach my hand out slowly and touch his head, he closes his eyes.

In that moment, something connects us.

*WHAT IS HAPPENING?!*

I hear the front door of the reception slam shut, the angry visitor has clearly given up and marched away.

Without any warning, there's a second flash of blue light and I shield my eyes with my arm. When I lower it, Silver is standing there again, watching me.

My breath caught in my throat, I find myself unable to move. Sitting at my feet, he tilts his head to the side, as though curious at my reaction. He nudges my leg with his nose. I'm too shocked to react, too freaked out to do anything. I stand there staring at him, a million questions flashing through my brain all at once.

A WOLF WAS RIGHT THERE.

*And I wasn't afraid.*

The door next to us swings open and Lucy and Dad appear, coming to an abrupt halt when they see Silver and I against the wall.

"There you are," Dad says, before he gives me a strange look. "Are you OK? You look … confused. Did you overhear that horrible man?"

"Don't worry about him," Lucy assures me. "Sometimes we get tricky visitors and hotheads! It's all part of the job. He's gone now."

"I'm afraid you can't take Silver home yet," Dad says, nodding to him still sitting patiently at my feet. "I thought you were putting him back in his kennel."

When I don't say anything, Dad reaches over to pat my arm. "Luna? What's wrong? Talk to me."

"I thought… I thought I saw…" I begin, trailing off. Looking down at Silver again, he stares back at me.

146

He's a dog. He's *definitely* a dog. I can see that. No question about it.

He is NOT a wolf.

I must have imagined it. That's the only explanation. I've been working at the rescue centre a lot recently, maybe this is what happens when you get over-tired – you imagine that dogs turn into wolves in a flash of light.

*There was no wolf.*

I shake my head.

"Sorry," I say, reaching down and stroking Silver's head. "I thought I saw something, but it was nothing. I'll put Silver back in his kennel and then we can go."

As I bend down to pick up Silver's lead, I see Dad shrug at Lucy, accepting my vague explanation. Leaving them waiting for me, I hurry back to Silver's kennel and lead him in, bending down to say goodbye before I shut him up for the night.

Stroking his head, I look into his eyes.

"I made it up, right?" I ask him. "I made it up in my head."

He sits down, exhales, and gives a slight bow of his head. Exactly like the wolf did.

*Weird.*

Straightening, I tell myself to stop being so ridiculous. There's no need to freak out right now. Silver is a dog, not a wolf. And he can't understand what I'm saying. He may appear to, but he can't. All dogs bow their heads like that sometimes. That's not a strange, unique occurrence. I'm clearly suffering some kind of episode due to exhaustion and potentially the warm weather we've been having. I may think I'm fine, but obviously I'm not. People who are fine do not hallucinate dogs turning into wolves.

I need to go home, get some rest, and I'll be laughing at this in no time. I lock up his kennel, and as I bid him goodnight, he looks up at me and gives a bark, but it's different to his usual bark, it's almost as if...

*It sounds like a wolf's howl.*

No. NO. I shake my head again. That was a *bark*. Definitely a bark. NOT a wolf's howl.

Because Silver is a dog. Not a wolf.

*Right?*

With one last glance at him over my shoulder, I rush out to meet Dad and Lucy. We say goodbye to Lucy as she gets in her car, and on the walk to Nan's house, I try my best to concentrate on what Dad is saying, although my mind keeps drifting back to the vision of Silver the wolf.

The smell of Nan's delicious homecooked stew hits me as soon as we step through the front door, and I try to act as though I'm hungry when she announces that it's ready to be served. I do everything as I would do normally – I take off my shoes and line them up neatly by the door; I help Dad set the table; I get a jug of water and I sit in my usual chair and tell Nan that the meal smells great.

"What's wrong, Luna?" Nan says as soon as she sits down, giving me a stern look across the table. "I can tell something is different about you."

HOW DOES SHE KNOW?!

"Nothing's wrong," I insist, trying to sound

upbeat and nonchalant. "I'm fine!"

"Come on, we don't have all night." Nan sighs, helping herself to salad. "What happened today that's caused you to come home all jittery?"

"Nothing!" I say, almost knocking over my glass as I reach for it. "It was a very normal day. Nothing strange happened at all. An average day of normal things. Just an average, normal day. Perfectly normal."

She narrows her eyes at me.

I clear my throat. "Anyway, Dad, you were saying you wanted to take Lucy on a date this weekend? That sounds like a good idea. Tell us about that."

"OK," he says slowly, giving me a strange look, before taking the hint and launching into a list of restaurant recommendations he's been given.

Nan may be suspicious, but my plan works, because no sooner has Dad mentioned two restaurants than she's telling him they're both terrible, and Mary from across the road had shocking food poisoning from the latter. Instead, she begins to give her recommendations, complete with explanations of their menus, chefs and ambiance, and I'm able to remain out of the spotlight for the rest of the meal, pushing my food around my plate and trying to build up an appetite.

After clearing up from dinner with Dad, I announce I'd like an early night and then run up the stairs, shutting myself away in my bedroom and leaning back against the door. I take a long, deep breath.

No matter what I keep telling myself, no matter how stupid it seems, I can't shake the image of the wolf out of my head.

There's no chance that Silver turned into a wolf.

*Is there?*

That night, I can't sleep. Tossing and turning in bed, I try to force myself to relax and forget about the day's unbelievable events, but nothing works. In the darkness, I stare up at the ceiling, my heart thudding against my chest.

I need to go back to see Silver. I have to know if what I saw was real. And to do that, I'm going to need a way into the centre and, potentially, a witness to make sure I'm not seeing things. There's one person who fits the bill.

Reaching for my phone, I scroll through my very short list of contacts and click on Kieron's name – I have the numbers of everyone who works in the rescue centre, in case of emergencies. He doesn't answer the first-time round, so I try calling him again and he finally picks up.

"Hello?" he answers, his voice groggy and confused.

"Kieron, it's Luna."

"Luna? What time is it?"

"Late," I whisper. "But I need your help."

"You do?" He sounds surprised. "Are you OK?"

"Yeah. I can't really explain right now, but I need you to meet me at the rescue centre."

"All right. When?"

"Now."

"*Now?* Are you serious?"

"Yes. Kieron, this is important. Something is going on, and I'm not sure if I'm seeing things, but … well, I need you to be there to make sure. No one else can know. That's why it has to be now so we can be there on our own. Will you help me?"

"Yeah, OK," he says.

"Thank you. You can't tell your mum. You'll have to sneak out of the house."

"That won't be a problem."

"Do you have keys to the rescue centre?" I ask hopefully.

"I know where she keeps them."

"And the alarm?"

"That also won't be an issue."

"Thanks, Kieron." I hesitate. "I really appreciate it."

"Sure."

"See you there."

Swinging my legs out of bed, I hang up, throw a jumper on over my pyjamas and pull on my trainers. I open my bedroom door as quietly as possible, listening out for Nan and Dad. I can hear soft snores from Dad's room and silence from Nan's.

Creeping across the landing, I gulp as I pass Nan's door, knowing full well that if she caught me trying to sneak out of the house, I would be in BIG trouble. I thankfully remember the one creaky step down the stairs and skip that one, pausing at the bottom to make sure the house is silent and still.

Grabbing the spare house keys from underneath one of Nan's boots, I tiptoe to the front door and wince at the clunk as I undo the lock, before stepping out into the cool night air, quietly closing the front door behind me. I wait by the house for a moment, and when no lights come on inside, I race as fast as I can down the road to the rescue centre. I don't have to wait too long until Kieron arrives wearing all black from head to toe, his heavy camera strapped around his neck and holding a notebook and pen.

"Why did you bring that?" I whisper, pointing to the camera.

"It sounded like you were going to reveal some kind of scandalous story going on at the rescue centre, so since I'm first on the scene, I thought I'd probably have to report on it. Is Chris at reception running some kind of money laundering scheme?

Is someone up to their neck in fraud? Or have you discovered some kind of long-lost treasure behind the door that's always locked in the cattery?" He gasps, his eyes lighting up. "OR a body?!"

"NO, there hasn't been a *murder*," I emphasize, horrified.

"What is it then?"

"You wouldn't believe me if I told you," I say. "Can we go in?"

He holds up the keys and I let him go ahead of me, carefully unlocking the several locks of the centre, before he types in the code to shut down the alarm. He gives me a sharp nod to let me know we're safe and I lead him straight to the kennels. The dogs are surprised to see us and start barking, but I am prepared for that, offering each of them a treat as we pass to quieten them down. Silver is waiting for me at his door, like he knew I was coming.

"Luna, what is going on?" Kieron asks impatiently, following us as I lead Silver back towards reception, away from the other dogs.

I don't answer him quite yet, waiting until we're in the quiet of reception and Silver has sat down next to me.

"OK, this is going to sound very strange," I begin, wondering if I'm doing the right thing by telling him. It's too late to go back now, anyway. Kieron would only keep digging until he got the truth. "But earlier I could have sworn... I think that... It seemed as though... Ugh, you're not going to believe a word I say!"

"Luna, whatever it is, you can tell me," Kieron says sincerely, frowning. "If you want, I'll put my camera and notebook away." He places them both on the reception desk. "See? This can be off the record. You can tell me whatever it is that's going on."

"OK. Don't laugh at me."

"I won't."

"Right." I take a deep breath. "Earlier, I think that Silver may have turned into a wolf."

He blinks at me. "Huh?"

"Silver turned into a wolf," I repeat. "There was a flash of blue light and suddenly, instead of a dog standing next to me, there was a wolf. A giant wolf.

156

Bigger than a normal wolf, I think. And after a few moments, there was another flash of light and he was a dog again."

Kieron hesitates. "Is this some kind of joke?"

"I'm not joking."

"This isn't some kind of set-up to make me look stupid?"

"No!"

"Because I know that you're not my biggest fan or anything, but to get me here in the middle of the night to pull a prank is a bit—"

"Kieron, I swear this is not a prank," I insist, getting irritated even though I know I'd react the exact same way if I was in his position. "I'm telling you the *truth*."

"You're saying that Silver, this dog right next to you now, turned into a wolf? Big fangs, claws, bushy tail. As in … a *wolf*."

"Yes."

He pauses. I stare right back at him with a dead-serious expression.

"Luna—" he begins, but I cut him off.

"Kieron, you have to trust me on this. I'm telling you that's what I saw, and I've spent the rest of the day wondering if I made it all up in my head, and that's why we're here now. I want to see if ... if it happens again. If it doesn't, then clearly I had some kind of strange hallucination."

"You want to try to see if he'll turn into a wolf now?" Kieron checks.

"Exactly."

"All right. Let's say that *somehow,* against all odds, this dog has the magical powers to turn into a wolf," Kieron says, looking at me strangely. "How does he do it? Because until you saw him do it tonight, he's never done it before."

"I don't know. That's what I want to work out," I admit, looking down at Silver quizzically.

I crouch down next to my dog, before hesitating and instructing Kieron to take a step back. He raises his eyebrows at me. I sigh, rolling my eyes.

"Just in case."

"Fine," he says, doing as I say and backing away.

"OK." I clear my throat, looking Silver in the eyes. "Silver? If you can understand me, which I think you might be able to, please can you turn into a wolf."

Nothing happens. Silver yawns and then has a good scratch behind his ear. Kieron looks pained as I try again.

"Silver, become a wolf!" I instruct.

He tilts his head at me. Nothing.

"Wolf, Silver! Wolf!"

Sill nothing.

"Three ... two ... one ... WOLF!"

Silver lets out a burp. I hear Kieron sigh witheringly behind me.

Blushing furiously, I run a hand through my hair. How could I have got so confused? How could I possibly have let myself believe for one second that something like this could be real? What. An. Idiot.

"I'm sorry, Kieron," I blurt out, my eyes brimming with tears of embarrassment. "I'm so stupid. This is mortifying. I shouldn't have bothered you. Let's forget it happened, OK? Please don't tell anyone. It's so embarrassing."

Kieron shifts his weight from one foot to the other. "No ... don't be embarrassed. There could be a perfectly reasonable explanation and I'm sure ... I'm sure you saw *something*."

"I want to pretend like this never happened."

"Luna—"

"Please?" I plead. "Just forget it."

He nods. "Sure."

"I'll go put Silver away and we can go home." I pause, quietly adding, "Thank you. For being nice about all this."

"Of course," he says gently.

I go to pet Silver, placing my hand down on the fur of Silver's back at the same time that we hear a car coming down the road.

A sudden flash of blue light fills the room and I get that strange warm, tingly feeling rush through me again, like I've turned into a giant sparkler.

When I open my eyes, a wolf is standing in

Silver's place.

Kieron lets out a yelp and stumbles backwards, tripping over his feet and falling on to the floor. He shuffles away from us on his bottom, his eyes wide with fear.

"WOLF!" he shrieks. "HELP! SOMEBODY, HELP!"

Kieron's reaction is normal, but again I'm not afraid. It's strange. I can't explain why I don't feel panicked. Maybe it's partly because I've seen the wolf before. But I think the main reason I feel a sense of calm is because of his eyes. They're Silver's eyes.

I could never be frightened of him.

"Silver?" I ask, crouching down slowly.

He looks at me and I can see in his gentle golden eyes that he's not going to hurt me. My heart racing, I start reaching my hand towards his head.

"L-Luna," Kieron whispers, horrified. *What are you doing?*

Ignoring Kieron, my fingers gently brush across the soft fur of the wolf's head. He bows his head and closes his eyes just like he did last time. His reaction encourages me to stroke his head properly and he lets out a small exhale of contentment. A smile spreads across my face.

"Hey," I say gently, scratching him behind the ears. "You're OK. No one's going to hurt you. I'm here."

In response, he brings his head forward and lowers his snout so that I can rest my forehead against his.

"Luna," Kieron squeaks. "Get away from it! What do you think you're playing at?"

"It's Silver," I confirm, glancing over to where Kieron is cowering. "You don't need to be scared. How is this possible, do you think? Could it be some kind of magic?"

"Luna, w-what has happened to your *eyes*?" Kieron gasps, staring and pointing at me in horror.

"What do you mean?"

"They … they've gone golden! L-like the wolf's eyes!"

With no idea what he's talking about, I fumble in my pocket for my phone and bring up my camera, turning it on to selfie mode and peering at my reflection on the screen. I almost drop my phone when I see it. My eyes, usually brown, have become as luminously golden as Silver's!

"*What is happening?*" I whisper, lowering my phone.

"I don't know, but I don't like this," Kieron croaks, his voice raspy. "There is a wolf right in front of you! Do you know how dangerous they are?! He could kill you! We have to get out of here! HELP! HELP!"

"Kieron, stop panicking. I'm telling you: it's Silver."

"That doesn't make any sense. It's … it's IMPOSSIBLE! Please listen to me and walk away from the wolf calmly. Don't make any sudden movements. We don't want to antagonize it!"

Before I can reassure him any further, we hear car doors slamming shut outside. The car that I'd heard coming down the road a moment ago has pulled up right outside the rescue centre. There are footsteps coming up the path towards the door.

"Uh-oh." I grimace. "Do you think our parents have realized we're here? Nan is going to kill me when she finds out."

"I think she may be slightly distracted by the WOLF!" Kieron hisses, staring wide-eyed at Silver still. "Luna, we have to GO!"

"Shush!" I hold a finger to my lips, returning my attention to the door.

I can hear low voices, but I don't recognize them. They're all male, but none of them are my dad. When I hear the sound of the lock being picked and the grumbling voice of one of the men saying, "Hurry up, would you, you utter plonker? We can't be seen!" all the blood in my body turns to ice.

"Kieron, I think the rescue centre is being broken into!" I whisper, turning to him urgently. "Hide!"

## CHAPTER NINE

"As if tonight couldn't get any worse!" Kieron whimpers. "I'm trapped with a wolf AND burglars!"

"Quick, Kieron, we have to hide!" I point at the reception desk. "Behind there! Hurry!"

*"I'm not going near a WOLF!"*

"Kieron, it's Silver!" I remind him, frantically glancing at the door. "He won't hurt you."

"How do you know?" he hisses back indignantly. "You've only met that wolf twice!"

"Come here now!" I instruct, ducking behind the reception desk with Silver. "Before they see you! Please! Trust me!"

Groaning, Kieron reluctantly crawls on his hands and feet across the floor to the reception desk and, without taking his eyes off Silver, quickly tucks himself beneath the counter as far away from us as possible. Silver ignores him, instead looking alert at the noise the intruders are making. When the door clicks open, Silver bares his teeth and emits a low warning growl. Worried that he'll give away our position, I hold my finger up to him.

Without saying anything, I'm willing him to be quiet and stay hidden. He glances at me and, as though he can read my thoughts, he immediately obeys, quietening and lowering his lip back over his teeth.

As the intruders come in, they switch on torches, the beams darting around the room as they make sure they're alone.

"Why hasn't an alarm gone off?" one of them says.

"Don't know, boss," another replies. "Chad, check it out."

"Why do I have to check it out?"

"Because I said so."

"You're not in charge, Dean."

"Neither are you, *Chad*. Callahan, who do *you* want to check out the alarm?"

"For goodness' sake, I'll do it," the man who must be Callahan snaps. There's a pause as he examines the alarm system on the wall by the door before he speaks again. "Strange. It looks as though the alarm isn't on. They must have forgotten to set it tonight."

Dean sniggers. "Lucky for us."

"Or someone is still here," Callahan remarks.

They fall into silence, and I suspect that they're listening out carefully.

Catching Kieron's eye, I hold my finger up to my lips. Shuddering, he hugs his knees to his chest.

"Guess you're right, Dean: it's our lucky night," Callahan continues eventually, apparently satisfied with not hearing any unusual sounds coming from anywhere else in the centre. "You definitely cut the wire of the CCTV camera outside, yes?"

"Oh yes," Dean says eagerly. "It was easy-peasy. And I was sure to park out of sight of that camera anyway, so they won't be able to see our van on any of the footage before it cut out."

"Good," Callahan replies. "Right, let's get this over with. Chad, come with me to the kennels. Dean, you stay here and keep watch."

"Gotcha, boss."

We hear their footsteps getting closer as two of them cross the reception area from the front door and, when they pass the desk, I can see that they're wearing masks to hide their faces from any cameras. As they reach the doors through to the next corridor, they stop.

"We won't be a minute, Dean," Callahan says. "I know exactly what I'm looking for."

I suddenly realize that's the second time someone has said that today, and it hits me that I've heard this Callahan guy's voice before. It's the man who came to the shelter and shouted at Lucy this afternoon when we were closed, I'm certain of it. He must have been hoping to scope out the kennels then.

Although it's scary that he was here earlier, working out a plan to return, this is definitely a good thing. It doesn't matter if they've cut the camera now, it means we'll have his face caught on the CCTV from earlier in the day.

They push through the doors that will lead them directly to the kennels, and I feel sick to my stomach – I won't let them hurt any of those animals. We have to do something. Taking a deep breath, and making sure that the spotlight of Dean's torch isn't beaming in my direction, I shuffle forward carefully and quietly out from where I'm tucked away under the desk and, ignoring Kieron's wide-eyed panic as he mouths "*What are you doing?*", I very slowly peer over the top of the counter.

Dean is pacing back and forth by the front door, humming to himself and looking bored. Lowering back down out of sight, I look around the reception area for inspiration. Watching me the entire time, Silver hasn't moved, remaining tucked under the desk where I left him, waiting for instruction. I spot the phone switchboard and a light bulb goes off in my brain. Dean has given up on the humming and has moved on to full-blown singing, albeit quietly. As he continues to entertain himself by launching into an old Elvis number, complete with dance moves, I reach towards the switchboard and press a couple of buttons.

As I'd planned, the phone in one of the veterinary rooms down the corridor starts ringing.

I duck out of sight again as Dean gasps, jumping at the noise and spinning around, the beam of his torch scanning across the reception desk before landing on the doors his companions went through earlier.

"Boss?" Dean whispers into the darkness. "That you?"

The phone continues to ring. He doesn't move, and eventually it rings out. I don't hesitate, pressing some more buttons on the switchboard so that the phone in yet another veterinary room starts going off.

"What's happening?" Dean asks out loud to no one, sounding panicked.

He decides to go check it out. I crawl back under the desk next to Silver, who puts one paw in front of me protectively as Dean comes blundering across the room, bashing through the doors to the corridor. When they swing shut behind him, I don't hesitate.

Getting my phone from my pocket, I call 999 and as soon as the operator answers, I tell her that the rescue centre is being burgled, giving her the address and begging her to send someone quick, before I hang up.

The phones in the veterinary rooms ring out and go silent, and in a matter of moments, Dean is back in reception. He is soon followed by the other two. Thankfully, they march straight past the desk to stand in the middle of the room, and I breathe a sigh of relief that they don't have any of the dogs or cats with them.

"What was that about?" Callahan demands.

"I don't know!" Dean says. "The phones started

ringing in those rooms down the corridor. I checked them out, but there's no one in there."

"Of course there's no one in there!" Callahan snaps. "If there was someone in there, they're not going to ring themselves, are they?"

"I thought it was a bit strange, though," Dean argues. "Who would be calling a rescue centre this time of night? Maybe it was someone who knew what we were up to, and they wanted to call here to warn someone!"

"They would call the police, you muppet," I hear Chad reply impatiently.

"Better safe than sorry, I say," Dean says huffily. "I was just checking. Did you find him, boss?"

"Does it look like I found him?" Callahan sighs. "No, he's not in there. Makes no sense – I saw the picture on the website. It looked just like him."

"Maybe it wasn't him. Dogs all look the same to me," Chad says.

"You what?" Dean sneers. "So, a little chihuahua looks the same as a Great Dane in your eyes, does it,

Chad? You need your eyes tested, mate."

"Shut up, Dean."

"You shut up, Chad."

"Both of you shut up!" Callahan cries, exasperated. "Do you know I am an award-winning scientist? I have worked with some of the best minds in the country! I should be famous by now! I should be being hailed for my discoveries! But what am I doing instead? I'm lumped with you two useless oafs scouring kennels nationwide looking for some overgrown fleabag! It makes me feel sick to my stomach!"

The others fall silent at his outburst.

In the distance, sirens are going off. They're getting closer. Kieron and I share a hopeful look.

"You hear that?" Callahan asks in a frenzy. "We have to get out of here."

"You see, Chad?" Dean spits. "I bet someone did rat us out after all, and it was something to do with those phones going off down the corridor."

"You couldn't be more of a blockhead if you tried, Dean," Chad retorts. "I'm willing to bet twenty quid on the fact that the two incidents are not related."

"You've got yourself a deal," Dean says.

"Shake on it," we hear Chad insist.

"Hang on," Dean says. "How will we work out if they're connected or not?"

"WILL YOU BOTH SHUT UP AND GET OUT OF HERE NOW!" Callahan roars, and I hear the front door squeaking open. "The sirens are getting closer! We need to leave! Dean, go start the van!"

"Yes, boss, at once," Dean says.

The door remains open for some reason, even though it should have shut behind them by now if they were rushing out.

I frown, listening out carefully before I move a muscle.

"Boss, what are you doing?" I hear Chad ask. "You said we have to go."

"Wait a minute! I've seen something very interesting," Callahan replies. "What do we have here?"

There are footsteps across the reception again and then the sound of paper ripping.

"What are you taking that for?" Chad asks.

"Because I've just found our answer," Callahan replies. "Now let's go."

I hear the door swing shut, followed by the sound of footsteps running down the path. Scrambling to my feet and ignoring Kieron's instructions to stay down, I rush out from behind the reception desk and dash across the floor to look out of the window as they climb into a waiting van, its engine already on thanks to Dean who's behind the wheel. I'm hoping to see the number plate, but it's parked side on to the centre and I can't see the plates on the front or the back. I can, however, make out a logo on the side of the van before they speed away, disappearing into the night.

I gasp as something dawns on me.

I've seen that symbol before. It's the same one that was stamped on the front of the top-secret folders that were among my mum's work things.

I jump as someone nudges me but realize it's Silver, who has been right next to me this whole time. I place my hand on his head. The police sirens are getting louder now.

"Are … are they gone? Is it safe?" Kieron asks from behind the desk.

"Yeah, they've gone," I assure him. "We need to get out of here before the police arrive."

"Why?" Kieron asks. "We need to tell them what happened!"

"And admit to breaking in ourselves? No, thanks. They didn't take any of the animals, that's the most important thing. We should leave the police to do their job – it's not like we can help much anyway."

"We can give the police their names," Kieron points out. "Although I don't really fancy explaining to my mum what we were doing here, especially when" – he glances down at Silver, still not completely at ease in his company but seemingly accepting that he's had a good chance to hurt us and hasn't – "well, I'm not sure how we would go about explaining that we were here to see if a dog could change into a wolf, and it turned out to be true."

"Let's go home and chat it through tomorrow.

Maybe we can work out a way of telling them why we were here that isn't quite so strange."

"Good plan." Kieron nods, before giving me a strange look. "Seriously, your eyes are so *weird*. Why have they suddenly changed? Do you feel any different?"

"I can't explain it. We'll talk about it later; we have to go. Don't forget your camera."

"Luna, wait!" Kieron says suddenly.

"The police have pulled up outside," I say, glancing out of the window. "We have to go."

"Quick! Look!" He points to the pinboard of staff photos and thank-you letters. "They may not have taken any of the animals, but they did take something. They took the photo of you and Silver!"

He's right. The picture is missing, the drawing pin that was sticking it to the board still in place with just a tiny scrap of the paper left.

"That's what the boss one must have ripped off before he left," Kieron says, looking confused. "Why would he have wanted my photo of you and Silver?"

"I have no idea," I whisper, stunned.

Mystified, we stand staring at the board until we're distracted by a flash of blue light that fills the room. We spin around at the same time as the light disappears to see Silver now back in his dog form. He barks at us, before looking at the door. I follow his eyeline to see two police officers strolling up to the centre.

"We have to go," I say.

"Your eyes! They're back to their normal colour!" Kieron shakes his head at me, completely aghast. "What is going on? Am I dreaming? Is this all a weird dream? Can you pinch me? Pinch me on the arm now, please. This can't be real."

"We have to *go*," I repeat, ushering him out of reception.

Kieron leads the way out the back, able to unlock all the exits with his set of keys.

"You need to put Silver back in his kennel," he says, noticing Silver remaining at my side as we leave through a gate round the back of the garden. "They'll notice he's missing."

"No chance," I tell him firmly. "It can't be random

that they took the picture of Silver with them when they left. Kieron, I'm scared that it's Silver who those people were after!"

His eyebrows knitted together, Kieron looks thoughtful for a moment and then finally nods in agreement.

"Maybe. If they know he's magical, then that could be why they want him. But what are you going to do with him?"

"What do you think? I'm going to take him home with me," I answer as Kieron locks the gate behind us.

"But what about your nan?" Kieron grimaces. "Won't she be angry?"

"Only if she finds out," I say nervously, resting my hand on Silver's head.

"You're going to sneak a dog that can turn into a wolf into your nan's house and keep the fact that he's staying with you a secret from her?" Kieron says to check he's got it right. Exhaling, he shakes his head.

"Good luck, I guess," he says. "You're going to need it."

"You think it will be that difficult?"

"Fooling a bunch of criminals is one thing," he says, turning to head home, "but fooling your nan is quite another."

# CHAPTER TEN

Sneaking Silver home isn't exactly easy.

The police must have contacted Lucy because I've just managed to creep into Nan's house and close the front door behind us, barely making a sound, when a light switches on suddenly upstairs. I usher Silver into the sitting room and we both hide behind the sofa as Dad comes barrelling down the stairs in his pyjamas, having just woken up, his hair sticking out all over the place. As he throws on a coat and pulls on his trainers, he's speaking into the phone.

"Don't worry; I'm on my way and I'll meet you there," he says, fiddling with his laces. "Tell the police I won't be long."

"Richard? What's going on?" Nan asks, coming down after him.

"There's been a break-in at the rescue centre," he tells her frantically, swinging open the front door and stepping out into the night. "Lucy's just spoken to the police!"

"Oh my goodness!" Nan cries, placing a hand on her heart and following him outside, the door closing gently behind her and resting on the latch. "Are all the animals OK?"

"She's gone over there now to check, and I said I'll join her," I hear Dad reply.

I take the opportunity of them both being outside to dart up the stairs with Silver, running as fast as I can across the landing and into my room, carefully shutting my door and leaping on to my mattress. Silver comes to sit patiently by the bed. I can hear Dad's voice drifting through the window from the driveway.

"Don't tell Luna anything yet; she'll only worry. I'll be back soon!"

"Let me know if there's anything I can do to help," Nan calls out after him, before coming back inside and shutting the front door.

I hear her come up the stairs and – to my horror – her footsteps get closer to my room. She's coming to check on me. With no time to do anything else, I lift the duvet, hiss at Silver to jump up on to the bed, and then I cover us both, my head slamming against the pillow. I shut my eyes just in time.

The door creaks open.

"Nan?" I say sleepily, opening my eyes to squint at her as she pops her head around the door. "Is it morning?"

"No, no, go back to sleep," she says quickly. "I was ... coming to say goodnight."

"Night," I yawn, shutting my eyes again.

The door clicks shut, and I breathe a sigh of relief as Silver pokes his nose out of the duvet and gives me a big lick on the chin. I grin at him.

"The things I do for you," I whisper.

He gratefully replies with another slobbery lick.

I think I'll find it hard to get to sleep, but the evening's events have clearly worn me out, because I drift off pretty much straight away and don't even hear Dad get home. Silver ends up climbing out from under the duvet and curling up at the end of the bed to doze off, which suits me just fine. It's nice to have the bed to myself, but I like knowing he's there.

In the morning, I turn over and gradually open my tired eyes to see his face looming right over mine, his front paws resting on my shoulders as he waits for me to wake up. I yelp as he licks me across the nose, pushing him off and bursting out laughing.

"Silver!" I giggle, wiping the slobber off my face. "Gross!"

"Luna? Are you awake?" comes Nan's voice from downstairs.

"Uh-oh." I groan at the sound of her stomping, quickly lifting the duvet and urging Silver to hide. "Quick! Under here!"

Luckily, he knows the drill, and jumps under it, lying down low next to me as I cover us both.

184

"Good morning," Nan says, bustling in with an orange juice as I make a big deal of stretching. "How did you sleep?"

"Great, thanks. You?"

"Fine. Time to get up and come down to breakfast. I'm afraid your dad's had a difficult night, but everything is OK," she says, coming to perch on the edge of the bed much to my horror.

"Oh no," I say, feigning surprise. "I'll come down now and then you can tell me all about it. Once I'm downstairs. You go, and I'll follow you."

"Don't be alarmed, but there was a break-in at the rescue centre," she says, looking at me in great concern. "But your dad has assured me that all the animals are fine."

"PHEW! That's good news. I mean, it's bad news about the break-in, but I'm glad everyone is OK. Anyway, if you go down to breakfast, I'll get up and join you. Let's get out of this room."

"Poor Lucy…" She sighs, shaking her head, not getting the message. "It's very distressing for her."

"Yes." I nod. "Very. Let's talk about it downstairs."

"I thought you all deserved a good breakfast this morning, so I've made *pancakes*."

Silver lets out a whine.

Nan starts at the noise, her eyes drifting across to where he's lying under my duvet.

"Hmmmmmmm!" I whine from the back of my throat, as high-pitched as possible to match Silver's tone.

"What is that noise you're making, Luna?"

"I'm just so excited about the pancakes! Hmmmmm! Yummmm!" I squeak.

She gives me a strange look. "Are you feeling all right?"

"Yes! I'm feeling great! So great that I want to get up and get ready for the day. So, shall I meet you downstairs for pancakes?"

"OK," she says, getting to her feet, still looking thrown by my behaviour.

"Can't wait!"

She glides across the room and leaves. I wait until the coast is definitely clear, and I can hear her downstairs in the kitchen chatting to Dad before I fling the duvet back and give Silver a stern look.

"You almost got us caught out there," I inform him.

He tilts his head at me.

"No more whining."

He tilts his head the other way.

"By any chance, did you whine because you heard the word … 'pancakes'?"

His eyes brighten and he licks his chops expectantly. I laugh, giving him a comforting pat on the head.

"Don't worry, buddy," I say. "I won't forget that you haven't had breakfast."

"Why would you want to take a pancake upstairs?" As he asks the question, Dad is staring me down across the table, his arms crossed, eyes full of suspicion.

"Why not?" I reply innocently. "It's fun to eat in your room!"

"You've already eaten two pancakes here," he points out. "Why would you want to take your last one upstairs?"

"No one is bringing any food upstairs," Nan says, jabbing her fork in my direction. "Don't think I don't know your secret, Luna."

I blink at her. "My s-secret?"

"Oh yes. You didn't think I'd work out that you have been nabbing cookies from the jar and taking them upstairs? I keep finding crumbs all over your bedding! If you can't manage to keep cookie evidence off your pillows, I'm not going to trust you to eat pancakes up there. If you're not careful, you'll end up like your great-aunt Abi."

"Why, what happened to my great-aunt Abi?"

"She had a habit of eating in bed, and one morning she woke up to find a mongoose had broken into her room and was lying on her head. Tried to suffocate her while she was sleeping."

"The mongoose did not try to suffocate her," I retort with a knowing smile. "It didn't know what it was doing. It's a *mongoose*!"

"Were you there, Luna Wolf? No. I'm telling you, she *swore* that mongoose knew exactly what it was doing. She never snacked in bed again."

"OK, fine," I say, letting out a heavy sigh. "I won't take a pancake up to my room. I thought it might be fun, that's all."

"You're not thinking straight this morning," Nan says, returning her attention to her breakfast.

"Maybe you didn't sleep very well and that's why," Dad adds, watching me curiously.

"She slept very well," Nan tells him. "She didn't even hear you leave last night."

"Yes, so she said."

I busily cut into the third pancake that I'm too full to eat and had been hoping to save for Silver. Maybe I can eat a bit of it and then stealthily pocket the rest somehow.

"So, you didn't hear me on the phone?" Dad asks me for the second time this morning. "You didn't hear me run down the stairs and leave the house. You didn't notice the light on the landing coming on or hear Nan and I having a conversation at the front door? And then you didn't hear me come back, either?"

"I must have been in a very deep sleep," I explain breezily.

"Yes. You must have been. Strange that you didn't hear so much going on, especially when I was so worried that I didn't exactly keep my voice down."

"Yeah, strange," I say, picking up my glass of juice to take a glug.

Dad rubs his chin. "It's almost as if you weren't in the house all night."

I choke on my juice, coughing and spluttering. Nan reaches out to thump me on the back.

"You all right, Luna?" she asks.

"Fine, the juice went down the wrong way, that's all," I reply, my eyes watering.

Taking the napkin Nan is holding out for me to dab my eyes, I look up to see Dad hasn't budged. In fact, it looks as though he was expecting some kind of dramatic reaction to his comment.

"I think I'm finished," I say, putting my knife and

fork down, leaving my third pancake barely touched. "Thanks so much, Nan, that was delicious."

As I get up to take my plate and cutlery, Dad clears his throat. "Luna, may I have a word with you?"

"Absolutely, go ahead," I say, putting my things away.

"I think it would be best if we speak in your bedroom," he suggests.

"What's this about?" Nan asks.

"Oh, nothing. Some house things I want to run past Luna," he explains, brushing her question aside with a wave of his hand.

"How exciting!" Nan beams at him. "Have you started looking at places? You know you can stay here as long as you need, Richard, it's a pleasure having you both."

"Thanks, Clementine, we love staying with you," he says, squeezing her hand and pushing back his chair to stand up. "Come on then, Luna, lots to discuss."

"Sure, sure." I nod. "How about we go sit in the garden and chat? Such a lovely day!"

"I'd rather we talk in your room. I think I've had

a bit too much sun recently."

"Or we could go chill on the sofa in the sitting room? We don't have to tackle the stairs after all those pancakes," I point out, forcing a laugh.

"I think your room is the best place for our little chat," he insists, giving me such a stern look that I know I'm not going to win this one.

I traipse up the steps ahead of him, praying that SOMEHOW Silver is going to be hiding away and out of sight. Before I get to my bedroom door, I spin around, blocking Dad on the landing to try to buy more time.

"My room is really messy," I say hurriedly. "Let's sit in yours."

Dad crosses his arms. "Open your door, Luna."

Grimacing, I turn back to my door and slowly open it. Silver is lounging on the bed. When he sees me, he lifts his head excitedly. I bury my head in my hands as Dad comes marching in after me and shuts the door behind us.

"*Luna!*" he hisses. "What were you THINKING?"

"I can explain!"

"You'd better! Do you know how worried Lucy and I were last night when we got to the rescue centre and Silver was missing?! We thought he'd been taken! We were so upset! Thank goodness I told Lucy I'd double-check he wasn't with you before we went into a full-on panic. Lucy was distraught at how you'd react!"

"Wait, you checked he was with me?" I ask, going over to the bed and plonking myself down next to him.

"I'm very glad I did!" Dad sighs. "I looked in on you when I got back last night and saw you sound asleep with Silver at the bottom of your bed. He came over to say hello to me."

"He did?"

"Yes, he jumped off the bed, wagging his tail and gave me a lick," Dad says. He softens as he gazes at Silver, before realizing he's supposed to be cross at me and getting all grumpy again. "Please explain to me why you thought it would be a good idea to keep Silver here when I explicitly told you that you weren't allowed to take him home until we moved out of Nan's!"

"I … I couldn't leave him there!" I say vaguely, still unsure as to whether I was going to admit I was there to witness the break-in. I needed to get my story straight with Kieron first, and I didn't want to drop him in it.

"So, you snuck him home? You know Nan doesn't allow dogs in the house!"

"Dad, please, I don't want him to stay at the rescue centre, especially when there's been a break-in. Please let me keep him here, please, please, please!"

"Luna," he begins, a little gentler, "you know we can't. It's not like he's far away when he's at the rescue centre and Lucy has already said that he's yours, so no one else will be allowed to adopt him. You can take him home once we have a place of our own."

"That might not be for months! He's a really good dog, perfectly behaved."

"He's still not meant to be here."

"Dad, I'm begging you," I say, putting on my best

puppy eyes and hoping Silver is next to me doing the same. "Help me keep this secret from Nan just for a little bit. If it really doesn't work out, then I'll take him back, but you never know, she might warm to the idea. We had a conversation recently and it did seem like she maybe wasn't as against it as she says. Please, Dad. *Please*."

His eyebrows knit together in what seems to be genuine turmoil as he looks from me to Silver and back to me again. He finally lets out a sigh, his shoulders slumping.

"Oh, all *right*," he says, giving in.

I jump up and run towards him, giving him a giant hug while Silver hops down after me and trots over to lick his hand. Dad can't help but laugh.

"I don't know whether this is a good idea," he says, stroking Silver's head. "But I can't seem to bear sending this dog back, even temporarily. There's something about him. Your mum would have adored him."

Silver whimpers and bows his head at that.

"Huh?" Dad says, raising his eyebrows. "It's like he knows what I'm saying."

"He has a habit of doing that," I say, reaching over to give Silver a tickle under his chin. "Trust me, Dad, you have no idea just how special this dog is."

"I'm sure I'll soon find out."

I hesitate. "Any chance you can do us a favour and get Nan away from the house so I can take Silver out into the garden or for a walk? He must need the toilet. You can message me when the coast is clear and then later when she's coming back so I can hide him again."

Dad sighs. "And so the chaos of having a secret dog begins! Let me think—"

"Richard? Luna?" Nan calls out. "Have you finished your chat?"

The colour drains from Dad's face as he realizes she's coming to the room.

"Quick! Hide Silver!" he says in a strangled voice.

I instruct Silver to lie down on the bed and once again cover him with my duvet, sitting directly in front of him while Dad hurries over to place himself next to me, the two of us hopefully blocking the strange lump under the cover.

Nan knocks on the door and opens it a smidge, before coming in properly.

"Sorry to interrupt, but I was—" She stops suddenly, her eyes narrowing at the duvet and I can hear Dad swallow a lump in his throat. "Luna Wolf, why haven't you made your bed yet?"

"Oh, yeah, sorry, Nan. I will in a minute."

"There are studies that prove making your bed increases productivity and focus throughout the day, and promotes a sense of calm," she states. "Not to mention it looks much nicer."

"I'll do it right away."

"Very good," she says. "Now, as I was saying, I'm sorry to interrupt, but I'm going to head to the shops in a minute to pick up some ingredients. I know we've just had breakfast, but it's important that you keep your energy up for the day, Richard, especially when you've had such a difficult night, so I'm going to make you a delicious cornmeal porridge for lunch. Does that sound OK?"

Silver whines hungrily beneath the duvet.

"Hmmmmmmmmmm!" Dad squeals over him as I desperately try not to laugh. "Sounds LOVELY!"

"Oh!" Nan looks bewildered at the noise that has emitted from Dad. "Uh … good. I'm glad. I'm not sure I've heard you react like that before, but I take it a loud whining is a good thing?"

"Yes, definitely. In fact, I'm so excited about that dish, I'd like to join you at the shops to get the ingredients!" Dad exclaims, jumping to his feet and ushering her out of the room.

"I can get it myself, Richard, no need for you—"

"I'd love to join you! What a fun excursion!" he continues, while I giggle at his enthusiasm. "Let's get going! I'm excited!"

"All right, if you insist," Nan says, heading down the stairs and getting her shopping bags ready.

"Luna, I will message you when we're on our way home," Dad announces as he follows her down.

"Great! Thanks, Dad," I yell down after him, grinning as Silver's nose pokes out from under the duvet. "You're the best!"

"Don't I know it?" he calls back, the front door slamming shut behind him.

# CHAPTER ELEVEN

In another life, I think Nan must have been a detective.

Keeping Silver a secret from her is proving to be incredibly difficult, and there is no way I'd be able to do it without Dad's help, so I'm actually really glad he knows.

Firstly, there's the matter of getting Silver out of the house every morning and back in every evening without Nan seeing. Dad has been using an array of impressively imaginative tricks like standing in the middle of the garden and yelling things like, "IS THAT AN ORANGUTAN?!" and then Nan will come running out to see if it really is an orangutan, while

Silver and I sneak down the stairs and out the front door.

Secondly, there's the question of unavoidable evidence that a dog is in the house, for example, the dog hairs and dirt from his paws. Dad and I are ON IT. Nan thinks I've become some kind of weird vacuum-cleaner fanatic since I'm using it so much in my room, but I'm constantly hoovering my duvet to make sure there's no trace left behind when we're out of the house on the off chance that she might come in to inspect my tidiness without my knowledge. Dad bought me a room spray too to "Cover the smell" he said, which Silver and I found greatly insulting, but reluctantly agreed was worth using.

I've been feeding him at the rescue centre every day, so I don't need to worry about hiding his food, but his water bowl needs to be stashed away at the back of my wardrobe every morning and fished out when we get back.

No matter how careful we are, I can tell that Nan is suspicious about something going on, even if she's not sure what it is. She's been watching me like a hawk when I'm around the house and asking all these probing questions, desperately trying to get to the bottom of whatever I'm not telling her. I've tried to act as naturally as possible, but it's not easy. When she asked Dad if he knew what was making me so distracted, he said that I'd been rattled by the rescue centre break-in, so that made her back off a little, but not much. She still pelts me with detailed and specific questions about my day over meals.

Keeping secrets from Nan is genuinely EXHAUSTING.

Since the break-in, things around the shelter have also been a bit different. Lucy was really upset about it and so grateful that none of the animals were harmed – she's barely left to go home she's been so worried. They've re-installed the CCTV and updated the locks, and the police have promised her that they're on the case, especially as they think it's the same gang who have been targeting several dog rescue centres but taking nothing with them.

Thanks to Kieron and I, the police do, at least,

have a strong lead: together, we worked out a way of telling them about Callahan without giving them the whole truth. If they knew we'd snuck out at night and were there at the same time as the intruders, they'd only worry. We had to make it seem as though we'd popped back a lot earlier for Silver and happened to see Callahan lurking about.

"Wait a second," Dad said, holding up his hands once I'd begun our explanation, "you're telling me that you came back to the rescue centre to get Silver and you saw this man … the one who had come by earlier and yelled at Lucy, scoping out the place?"

"Yep." I nodded vigorously. "He was checking out the wiring of the CCTV camera."

"And … and I heard him say, 'I'm going to come back here tonight and rob the place!'" Kieron added, gaining himself a pointed look from me as, personally, I thought that was a bit overkill.

Lucy looked at Kieron in disbelief. "You overheard him *say* that?"

"Yes, he was talking to his cronies," Kieron

said confidently.

"His cronies," Lucy repeats.

"Two guys in face masks."

"They were wearing face masks at that point?" Dad frowns in confusion.

I nudge Kieron in the ribs to try to get him to shut up.

"What Kieron means is we couldn't see their faces because they were in a car," I said hurriedly. "But they were acting very suspiciously, and one of them called the man 'Callahan', so we know that's his name."

"And, Kieron, you were there to help Luna unlock the doors to get Silver?" Lucy said, crossing her arms. "I don't remember you leaving the house that afternoon after the party."

"I was very stealthy, Mum," he insisted, glancing at me. "Like a ninja, me. Right, Luna?"

"Very stealthy," I agreed. "We were in and out of there very quickly and home before either of you knew it."

"Uh-uh," Dad said, sharing a look with Lucy.

"Don't ever do that again, right? Imagine if you'd been at the rescue centre when it got broken into."

"Imagine," Kieron said, shuddering.

"Thank you for this information; we'll tell the police. But no more secrets from now on with you two," Lucy said, pointing her finger at us. "Promise?"

"Promise," we chorused, crossing our fingers behind our backs.

I know it's bad to lie, but it's not like we can casually drop into conversation that Silver has the magical ability to turn into a wolf. They wouldn't believe us for a start, and if by any chance they did, they might take him away from me. I can't take that risk.

Witnessing a break-in together – not to mention the magical transformation of my dog – has kind of unexpectedly created a weird bond between Kieron and I. He's started randomly showing up at Nan's house to fill me in on his research that he's been getting stuck into, reading up on animal genetics and scientific breakthroughs to try to track down a reasonable explanation. He's not had much luck there, so he has turned to myths and legends.

When I first met him, I found his persistent questions about Mum a bit rude, but now we're in this together and I'm getting to know him a bit more, it's actually really nice to be able to talk about something so baffling with someone who is as fascinated by it all as I am. He has this amazing determination to find out what's going on, and he's not afraid to dig around for the truth and ruffle feathers. I wish I had that kind of confidence.

I'm finding myself slowly starting to enjoy his company.

"It's impossible," he says, three days after the break-in as we watch Silver play fetch with a tennis ball in the garden area. "But I saw that dog turn into a wolf with my own eyes. There has to be a reason."

"It must be … magic."

"Yeah, OK, but even so, what sparks the transformation off? What made him turn into a wolf at that moment and then back into a dog? What was that flash of blue light? How do we know it's not going to happen in front of Mum and your dad? And he's been in the centre for months – why is it suddenly happening now?"

I sigh, offering him a small smile. "You ask so many questions, Kieron."

"Someone has to," he replies simply. "That's why the world needs investigative journalists like me."

Despite all his questions, he's yet to reach any answers and is getting increasingly frustrated, so instead I suggest that he start looking into the logo that was on the side of the van. That could be a clue too. He is dubious and points out that the van may have been stolen, but I insist he looks into it without revealing it was on my mum's files. I want to work out what it is first before I tell him that she may have been somehow involved.

The following day, when I'm helping with the grooming of a chow chow at the shelter, Kieron comes into the room and asks if I'd like to go for a walk in the park with Silver, giving me a look that means I should say yes. Once we're through the gates of the park, Kieron gets out his phone and shows me a picture of the symbol on his screen.

"You found it!" I exclaim.

"I think so, although it took a lot of digging, and there's so much secrecy surrounding this thing," he says, examining the picture. "The only way I could find it was to get into the National Archives and look through their records for dissolved companies. But someone has wiped all the information that goes with it – name, the nature of business, the registered office address, named directors and shareholders – there is NOTHING explaining what it is. I'm surprised the logo is still in existence on there. Someone must have wanted to keep hold of the logo and not let anyone else use it, in case they want to start it up again in the future, but at the same time stop anyone from finding out any information about the company's previous work."

"So, you don't know anything about it?"

"No. I had to trawl through hundreds of company logos to come across it, but I wanted to make sure with you that this is definitely the right one before I go any further with my research."

I take his phone in my hand and examine the picture closely, before nodding.

"Yes, that's the one. That was the symbol on the van."

"OK, well, it's a start," he says triumphantly. "I'll see what I can find out about it."

"Thanks, Kieron. I mean it. I really appreciate your help on this."

"A question for you, though, Luna: even if we do find out that this logo belongs to some kind of corporation or criminal organization, what then? Do we tell the police?"

"I guess so. They haven't managed to track down anything about that Callahan guy, though, not even with facial recognition. He doesn't seem to exist."

"I think if we found Callahan, we'd find all the answers, maybe even to Silver's magic," Kieron says thoughtfully. "Why else would he take that picture off the wall? He must know about him."

I instinctively grip Silver's lead tighter. "If he

does, then Silver has made it very clear that he doesn't like him. He growled when he sensed Callahan at the centre."

"That was when he turned into a wolf."

"Yes."

"And then when Callahan came back there that night, Silver turned into a wolf again," Kieron says, his forehead creasing. "It can't be a coincidence."

"You think Silver and Callahan are connected by the magic?"

"I don't know." Kieron sighs. "We're talking about a magical dog here. I don't know *anything*."

I can't help but laugh, and Kieron starts chuckling too.

"Either way," he continues, "I'm really glad you trusted me with this secret, Luna, and that it was me you came to for help." He looks down at Silver admiringly. "The whole thing is pretty cool, even if it makes no sense."

"I'm glad I told you too," I admit, and then get a wave of guilt about holding anything back from him.

If he's doing all this work researching the symbol,

he deserves to have the whole truth. Either I trust him, or I don't. I decide to trust him.

"Kieron, there's something else you need to know," I blurt out.

"Please don't tell me that the chow chow turns into a golden bear or something."

"No." I giggle. "Although that would be AMAZING. No, it's about my mum."

He looks at me curiously. "What about her?"

"Nan gave me some of her things last weekend, and there were these files. They were empty, but I think they were something to do with her work. They had 'Top Secret' stamped across them."

"Wow!" He looks impressed. "Was your mum a *government spy?*"

I shake my head. "No, not a spy. She was a scientist, remember?"

"Scientists can make awesome spies."

"My mum wasn't a spy," I clarify, trying to keep him focused. "The reason I bring it up is because the top-secret files had that logo on them. The same as the one on the van."

Kieron stops abruptly in his tracks. "Are you sure?"

"Yes," I say quietly, my eyes dropping to the ground. "Sorry. I was worried to tell you."

"Why?"

"Because … it's a bit weird, isn't it? That my mum has files with that symbol on them among her things. The same symbol on the van of criminals. What does that mean?"

"It could mean anything," he reasons. "You shouldn't jump to any bad conclusions. Let me check it out and see what I can find. It could be a wild coincidence."

"I'm not sure any of this is a coincidence."

Falling into silence and lost in our thoughts, we carry on with our stroll through the park. Silver is happily trotting along next to me, sniffing the grass and wagging his tail, enjoying his walk, until he suddenly stops.

"Silver, come on," I say, tugging on the lead.

But he won't move. Instead, he ducks his head to the ground as though he's on the prowl, stares straight ahead and lets out a low, threatening growl.

"What's wrong with him?" Kieron asks, putting his hands on his hips. "Does he want to go home?"

"No, he doesn't ever get tired," I point out, following his eyeline down the path ahead of us.

"Has he seen a squirrel or something?"

"Or someone," I muse, acknowledging that the park is pretty empty apart from three figures approaching us down the path. "Kieron, look."

He squints at the three people. "What?"

"Those three men coming towards us, they're wearing all black."

"So?"

"So, think about why Silver growled before."

Kieron's eyes widen in alarm as he realizes what I'm getting at.

"You don't think that might be" – he audibly gulps – "Callahan and his cronies?"

The three men are speeding up towards us now, and since they're not wearing masks this time, we can see their faces. The man leading them has blonde curly hair and glasses and something about him seems weirdly familiar, as though I've seen him somewhere before but can't place him. I notice one of the men at the back is holding what could be mistaken for a lead from a distance, but now that they're closer, it looks more like a dog-catcher pole: a long silver handle with a hoop at the end.

"Luna, we should go," Kieron says, nudging my arm. "They're looking straight at us. I think you might be right."

"Yeah," I say, turning with him and pulling on Silver's lead.

But Silver is staring intently at the three men, his teeth fully bared, too focused to be dragged away.

"Silver, we need to go," I say, tugging on the lead with all my strength, but he won't budge, and they're getting closer and closer. It's as though he can't hear me.

In an attempt to distract him, I repeat his name and reach forward, putting my hand on his back and—

A flash of brilliant blue light fills the air.

Silver is now a huge wolf, standing tall in the

middle of the park, his fangs on full show, his ears pricked up and forward. The three men stop. The two at the back gasp in disbelief. A wide, crooked, victorious smile spreads across the face of the man in glasses at the front.

"At last!" he cries, punching the air. "We've found him! We've found the last one!" He turns to the two men. "Dean! Chad! Capture them! The girl and the wolf! NOW!"

Silver crouches lower to the ground, his bushy tail swishing side to side, his golden eyes focused on the two men who are running right at him, one of them holding the dog-catcher pole aloft threateningly. Silver doesn't even blink. He starts barking at them, drool dripping from his fangs.

Dean and Chad both slow right down, suddenly deciding that the best way to capture a wolf probably isn't to run right at him.

"Stay away from us!" I shout at them angrily, Silver barking along with me.

"Hand over the wolf," one of them demands.

"Yeah! Do as Chad says, and no one has to get hurt," Dean adds, holding the pole out.

"I wouldn't come any closer if I were you," Kieron says. "In case you didn't notice, that right there is a wolf. A *ferocious* wolf!"

"Did you know that wolves can prey on large animals like elk and moose?" I tell them, thankful for the wolf book I got from the library. "Yeah, you heard me. This guy can take down a big MOOSE. You think *you're* any kind of match for him?"

Dean and Chad share a worried glance.

"Stop hanging about and CATCH THEM!" the man in charge, who must be Callahan, orders them.

"The others weren't in their magical forms when we caught them!" Dean points out as Silver snarls at him. "This one may take a bit more time, boss!"

"I don't care what it takes! Get him!"

"Dean! Get the loop around his head!" Chad instructs.

"You distract him then!" Dean squeaks, gripping the pole with two hands.

Chad nods and then reaches into his pocket and pulls out a handful of dog treats. "Here, you scruffy mutt!"

He scatters the treats on the ground. Clenching my fists, I will Silver to stand up to these bullies. Ignoring the treats, Silver leaps into action. With a loud howl, he pounces in Chad's direction. Chad screams at the top of his lungs, stumbling and falling to the ground.

"GET HIM, DEAN! HELP! HELP!" Chad squeals, scrambling backwards on his bottom as Silver rushes at him.

Dean lunges at Silver with the pole, managing to get the loop around Silver's neck. Without thinking, I run at Dean and jump on him, the surprise causing him to drop the pole completely. With a roar of frustration, Dean shakes me off, and I land on the grass with a thud. As he rounds on me, Kieron comes out of nowhere and swings his backpack at him, knocking him across the head.

"OOF!" Dean cries, his hands flying to his forehead as he trips over his feet, toppling backwards on to the ground and landing next to Chad.

Silver has managed to shake the loop from around his head and, grabbing the pole within his jaws, he holds it up and moves to tower over Chad and Dean before he snaps it clean in two.

Propped up on their elbows, Chad and Dean look at each other in horror before turning back to Silver and both letting out blood-curdling screams. Scrambling to their feet, they run away at full pelt in the opposite direction.

"WHAT ARE YOU DOING?" Callahan roars after them. "Get back here and catch that wolf!"

"Catch him yourself," I challenge as they ignore him, and Callahan is left alone to look back at the three of us.

Silver crouches to the ground again, ready to pounce.

Callahan's eyes widen in fear, and he starts walking backwards.

"You haven't seen the last of us," he warns. "That *magic* belongs to me."

And with that he spins on his heel and sprints away, disappearing into the distance.

## One Year Ago

# A SECRET ANIMAL KINGDOM IN HERTFORDSHIRE:

## SURPRISE ARRAY OF PETS DISCOVERED AT INJURED JOURNALIST'S HOME

Exclusive report for the *Daily Bugle*
*By Truffle Trilby*

Yesterday morning, a Hertfordshire ambulance crew were surprised to be greeted by a variety of wonderful animals when they were called out to help local journalist Rex Robinson.

Mr Robinson suffered a broken foot after it was, allegedly, trodden on by a donkey who had come wandering into his kitchen. When paramedics arrived at the scene, they did not just come across the many rescue donkeys Mr Robinson looks after on his sprawling country estate, but also a variety of dogs and cats, not to mention a ferret, a gecko and a sparrow, all of whom appeared to live at the house.

"At first I thought the ferret was a giant white rat," paramedic Phil Bell admitted. "Couldn't get it to stop jumping around on my head, it was quite annoying actually. Then a green lizard ran up my arm and I almost had a heart attack, but Mr Robinson assured me it was very friendly. The bird seemed a bit snooty, to be honest. It didn't come and say hello."

Despite Mr Robinson asking Mr Bell and his colleague not to tell anyone about the animals, Mr Bell believes Mr Robinson is being modest and thinks it's nice for people to know how kind he is to have taken in so many abandoned animals.

"Rex Robinson has always kept himself to himself," said a neighbour. "He used to be a very important investigative journalist, but I don't think he has written anything in years. I had no idea he kept all these animals! What a strange man!"

Mr Robinson is currently in hospital being treated and did not reply when we contacted him for comment.

As the van pulls up at the large, wrought-iron gates of Rex Robinson's house, Callahan lowers today's newspaper having read the article about Rex's broken foot several times over. Dean parks and turns off the engine. It's late – they've waited until the cover of darkness to drive here.

"Is this it, boss?" Dean asks, peering out of the window down the long driveway.

"This is it," Callahan confirms, before swivelling to look at Chad. "You double-checked with the hospital that Rex Robinson is still there? He hasn't been discharged?"

"I'm telling you, boss, he's at the hospital," Chad assures him. "According to the nurses, he's causing no end of trouble trying to get home, but he hasn't got out yet."

"Good." Callahan smirks. "Poor old fool. Come on, let's get this over with. One of you climb over the gate and press the button to let us in."

"Dean, you do it," Chad says.

"Why do I have to do it?" Dean huffs.

"Because you're the better climber out of the two of us," Chad insists. "You're much more flexible than I am."

Dean hesitates and then can't help but smile. "Aw. Thanks, Chad."

He hops out of the car and starts hoisting himself up the gate, while Chad snickers away in the van.

"Can't believe he fell for that. What an idiot,"

he says smugly, watching as Dean struggles to pull himself up and over.

He gets to the top eventually, swinging his leg over and then attempting to carefully lower himself down the other side, but his feet slip and his legs flail about hopelessly as he hangs from the top of the gate before he falls, landing with a loud thud on the ground, much to Chad's delight.

"Hurry up and let us in!" Callahan barks impatiently from the van, rolling his eyes.

Dean groans in pain as he rises to his feet and dusts himself off, limping to the side of the gate and pushing the buzzer.

"What are you hanging about for? Get back behind the wheel!" Callahan instructs Dean as the gates begin to open.

Focusing on the day he gets to lie on a beach in Mexico somewhere to make all this worth it, Dean hobbles back to the van and climbs into the driver's seat.

"Very smoothly done," Chad says, sniggering.

"Oh, shut up, Chad, at least he helped. You did

nothing," Callahan snaps.

Dean smirks at a sulking Chad triumphantly in the rear-view mirror.

They crawl down the driveway, marvelling at Rex Robinson's house as they park up outside. On Callahan's instruction, they get the tranquilizer, cages and animal-catcher poles from the back of the van, before they each take a torch and begin canvasing the outside of the house. The gravel crunches under Callahan's shoes as he treads around the side of the building, carefully shining the light of the torch through each window he passes before he finds what he's looking for.

He gasps with joy as he sees a snoozing white ferret in the sitting room. The beam from his torch scans the room and passes over an orange tabby cat curled up in an armchair, a large brown and white dog on the rug by the fireplace, a small green gecko tucked under what looks like a large log that has been purposefully placed for him on top of a table, and a sparrow sleeping soundly in a beautifully handcrafted bird box on the mantelpiece.

Callahan can't believe it. All these years, they've been hiding here with this reclusive journalist, no doubt the man who helped Athena escape with them six years ago. If that paramedic hadn't unwittingly spilled the beans on their whereabouts to a reporter, they may never have found them. As soon as Callahan and his boss read that article spelling out the exact location of the animals that they were looking for...

Well, their hope has been realized. Here they all are. Waiting to be captured.

"At last. *I've found them*," Callahan whispers. "Chad! Dean! Get over here, you idiots!"

"Want me to smash the window?" Dean offers, sidling up to him.

"No, they'll be harder to catch once they're awake," Callahan replies in a hushed voice. "We need to try to do this as quietly as possible. Get the gecko, the bird and the ferret first – they're harder to catch. Once they're in cages, we can always get the dog and the cat with the tranquilizer darts. They're bigger and easier targets."

"Got it." Chad nods, before quietly testing each window of the room. His face lights up as he reaches the final one on the right. "This one has a loose latch!"

He quietly opens the window, pulling it up high enough so that they'll easily be able to climb in.

"You think there will be an alarm?" Dean whispers.

"The man had a broken foot. I doubt he had time to hang about and set an alarm," Callahan reasons. "A neighbour has probably been popping in to feed the animals. It's unlikely, but if one goes off, like I said, focus on capturing the little critters before targeting the bigger ones."

Chad goes first, ducking his head to climb through the window, and giving the others a thumbs up once he's in the room and no alarms have gone off. Dean passes him all the cages and poles, before climbing in after him, followed by Callahan. Callahan rubs his hands with glee and then points at Dean to get the ferret and Chad to go for the gecko, while he elects himself to get the bird. He doesn't trust those two clumsy oafs to attempt to seize anything with wings. Such a feat is no doubt beyond their talents.

Once they've picked their way across the room to their various stations and are holding their cages at the ready, Callahan gives them a nod.

Quick as a flash, the three of them successfully manage to sweep the animals into the cages and lock them in before they wake up and realize what's going on. At the sound of the clicking locks, the dog's head jerks up.

His golden eyes fix on Callahan.

Leaping to his feet, his hair standing on end, he begins barking his head off. The cat jumps in fright at the disturbance, but Chad has already made his way across to her. As she leaps up, he grabs her. With a loud hiss, she begins to scramble within his grip, claws out, fighting against her capturer with all her might.

"YEEEEEOOOOOWWW!" Chad cries in agony as she sinks her claws into his face. "DEAN! GET A CAGE NOW!"

Grabbing another cage, Dean comes rushing over,

and the two of them manage to get the cat in, but not before she's left deep scratch marks all over Chad's face and arms. Dean bursts out laughing at his companion.

"You deserve that after making me fall off the gate!" Dean sniggers.

"I didn't *make* you fall off the gate!" Chad cries. "That was your own stupidity!"

"Shut up, Chad!"

"Shut up, Dean!"

"BOTH OF YOU SHUT UP AND HELP ME!" Callahan barks in terror.

He's currently being backed into the corner of the room by the large, snarling dog, who is creeping towards him, head low, teeth bared, ready to pounce.

"Get the tranquilizer gun!" Chad orders Dean, while he reaches for the dog-catcher pole.

The dog turns his head towards their commotion, and his eyes widen at Dean loading the dart into the tranquilizer gun. Without a moment's hesitation, he starts leaping around the room. Chad chases after him with the pole, banging into the chairs and tables dotted around the room, bashing his knee on the grand piano as he races past it. He howls in pain.

"Get him with the tranquilizer, Dean!" Callahan orders.

Dean aims the gun and starts to shoot the darts, but the dog is too quick, dodging all of them as he leaps around the room, trying his best to knock against the cages of his fellow animals as he goes, as though he might be able to loosen the locks that way and set them free, but it doesn't work.

"Aim, you useless dimwit!" Chad huffs at Dean, watching in despair as darts litter the walls. "You are such a terrible—" He is interrupted by a dart striking him in the bottom.

"Whoops," Dean winces. "Sorry, Chad."

"You little—" Chad begins, but passes out before he can finish the sentence, landing flat on his face on the floor.

The dog takes advantage of the distraction and jumps through the open window.

"NOOOOOOO!" Callahan cries, hurrying

across the room.

He leans out of the window and peers through the darkness. It's too late. The dog has run away, and there's no sign of him. Callahan sighs, closing his eyes in irritation, before he takes a deep breath and pulls himself together.

No matter. He has captured the other four. He wasn't sure he'd ever see these animals again and now he successfully has the majority of them back in his care.

"Load up the van," he tells Dean, turning round to see him poking an unconscious Chad with his foot.

"Sure thing, boss," Dean nods, putting away the tranquilizer gun and picking up two of the cages. "What about the dog?"

"Don't worry about the dog; we'll find him eventually." Callahan smirks confidently, looking back out of the window. "He can't hide for ever."

# CHAPTER TWELVE

Kieron has been coming over to Nan's every day to help me sneak Silver out for his daily walks. After the incident in the park, we agreed we should stick together whenever Silver had to leave the house, in case Callahan and his men tracked down where I was keeping him. Since that day, Silver has remained in his dog form, so Kieron and I have guessed that he only turns into a wolf when he senses danger. We've been on high alert, but luckily we haven't seen any sign of Callahan.

One afternoon, I hear the now-familiar sounds of Kieron knocking on the front door, greeting Nan as she lets him in, and then his footsteps as he comes running up the stairs. I hop off the bed and open my bedroom door for him, while Nan returns to her gardening outside.

"You're early," I remark as Silver's tail happily thumps against the mattress on seeing Kieron enter the room. "I thought we were going to go for a walk later when Nan meets her speed-walking group."

"Ah! That explains her neon-orange headband and matching legwarmers," Kieron says, throwing his backpack down on the floor. "Not many people can pull that off, but your nan sure has style. Anyway, I had to come and see you now."

"Why?"

"You should sit down."

I nervously follow his advice, perching next to Silver and absent-mindedly placing my hand on his head.

"What's going on?"

Kieron opens his backpack and retrieves a print-out which has the familiar logo of the letter "M" within the set of jaws in the centre of the page and the word "**MAGNITUDE**" written beneath it in a bold black font. He holds it out for me to examine.

"What is this?" I ask, clutching it in my hands and looking up at him in confusion.

"After hours of investigating that logo, I was getting nowhere," he informs me, putting his hands on his hips, his eyes red from tiredness. "I managed to hack into certain veterinary pharmaceutical and science companies' private message boards, but even there I couldn't find anything that—"

"Wait, you're able to *hack* into sites?" I ask, impressed.

He shrugs, as if it's no big deal. "If you want to investigate things, you need to be willing to dig in places where people don't want you to dig. I've been an accomplished hacker for several years now. I'm pretty sure I might have made one of the British Secret Service lists of 'ones to watch'."

I blink at him. "Wow."

"Anyway, the point is, I wasn't getting anywhere, so I started to post on some of those message boards, asking questions about the logo, but I either got no answers or people replied saying they'd never seen it before." He pauses, his eyes widening with excitement. "And then an email lands in my inbox from someone saying they'd seen my questions and asking me why I'm interested in the logo."

"Who was the email from?" I ask, intrigued.

"It was anonymous," he tells me. "And the email address was untraceable."

"Did you reply?"

"Of course." He nods. "I said that I was an investigative journalist who'd got a tip about the logo being recently spotted at the sight of a rescue centre break-in and I was trying to see if it was in any way connected. I also mentioned that I was trying to work out the involvement of someone who went by the name of 'Callahan'. Guess what happened?"

I lean forwards apprehensively. "What?"

"They replied with an unpublished article about 'Magnitude', a top-secret science project that was privately funded by some anonymous wealthy benefactor!" He reaches over to tap the symbol on the piece of paper I'm holding. "Luna, if this logo was on your mum's files, I think she might have been one of the scientists working on Magnitude."

"I've never even heard of Magnitude!" I exclaim, staring at the logo.

"It was shut down seven years ago and all evidence of the project wiped from the records. That's why I couldn't find any information on it. Someone did a very good job of trying to wipe its existence altogether. And the mystery person who sent me this article? They wrote in the body of the email that I was on the right lines to be asking questions about 'Callahan' – according to them, a Dr Gerry Callahan was one of the scientists behind Magnitude."

"Dr Gerry Callahan," I echo in a whisper. "We overheard him boasting about being a scientist during the break-in at the rescue centre! It must be the same person!"

"His existence has been wiped from the internet, though," Kieron tells me. "I googled him as soon as this email came through. There are no records, no social media, nothing on Dr Callahan. I think whoever he is, he's hiding his tracks and he's done it very well. That's why the police weren't able to find him."

I run a hand through my hair. "The criminal ringleader who has been terrorizing rescue centres and searching for Silver is one of the scientists from Magnitude. And my mum was his ... colleague?"

A light bulb goes off in my head. I jump to my feet and crouch down to pull the box of Mum's things out from where I'd stowed it away under my bed. Rummaging through it, I locate the ripped photo I found and pass it to Kieron.

"That's Callahan!" I exclaim, jabbing my finger at the blonde man in the glasses and lab coat standing next to Mum. "I didn't put two and two together at first, but if you take away the moustache he has here – it's definitely him! I thought he looked familiar."

"So, they *were* colleagues," Kieron says, aghast.

My heart sinks and I slump on to the bed. Sensing something is wrong, Silver whimpers in solidarity and moves to rest his head on my lap.

"This is not good news," I say drearily. "What was my mum doing working with someone like Callahan? I don't understand! What was Magnitude and why did it shut down?"

"I'm glad you asked," Kieron says, brimming with excitement. "According to the article I was sent, the project was instantly terminated when a scientist working there realized that those funding Magnitude had lied to them about the use of their research. The scientist decided to do something about it, so they spoke to this journalist and suddenly" – he claps his hands, making Silver and I jump – "the project was shut down. Just like that."

"But, Kieron," I begin impatiently, "what was the project in the first place?"

Kieron takes a deep breath. "The people at Magnitude had somehow found a way of enhancing domestic animals using some kind of powerful energy source. Luna, they had found a way of making them *super-animals*."

We both look down at Silver, who decides that this

is the perfect moment for a good scratch, his hair flying everywhere as he clumsily scratches behind his ear.

"So, what you're saying," I croak, my mouth dry, "is that Silver…"

"Silver is one of those animals, yes," Kieron finishes when I run out of words, too overwhelmed by this information to process it properly. "Magnitude had been successful at transforming five animals in total before everything was shut down and the animals were taken by this whistleblowing scientist to a secret safe location."

"That's … wild!"

"Do you remember when we were in the park and Callahan and those idiots mentioned how the others they'd captured weren't in their magical forms?" Kieron recalls. "How Silver was the last one? I think they found that secret location, and they managed to get them all back, except…"

He trails off.

"Except for Silver," I say in disbelief.

"That's why they're looking for him. They know

exactly what he can do," Kieron says, his forehead creased with concern. "That's why they didn't take any animals from those rescue centres they broke into. They were specifically looking for the last super-animal. When they saw Silver on our website, they must have recognized him and realized they'd finally tracked him down."

I reach over to the photo of Mum in the frame on my bedside table.

"Kieron, do you think this is Silver with my mum?"

"It makes sense," he says, peering down at it. He suddenly gasps. "And you know what else makes sense now that I look at this picture? Why Silver has such a connection to you! He obviously loved your mum. Maybe he could sense that you were her daughter!"

"Do you really think so?"

"That explains his attachment to you and only you! The moment you walked into the rescue centre, he knew exactly who you were. Silver belongs to you because he belonged to your mum!"

"But Silver *hates* Callahan. And Callahan worked

alongside my mum. Why would he hate one scientist but love another?"

Kieron looks pensive for a moment as he considers my question, before clicking his fingers. "The scientist that leaked the story! What if that was your mum? The people behind Magnitude hired the best and brightest scientists who specialized in animals and their welfare, persuading them that they had discovered this incredible magical source that would elevate medicine for animals. It would help to cure disease and health issues; it would save countless animals' lives. They just needed the right people to work with it and make that happen. People like your mum."

"It does sound like something she'd be interested in."

"But then, what if she found out that was never Magnitude's intention? What if she found out that she, and a lot of her colleagues, had been duped? That the powers-that-be had used her talent, intelligence and passion for animals to develop a product that wouldn't be used to help them, but instead would turn the animals into something more for their own financial gain – for example, an extremely rare and precious dog that could turn into a wolf. How would she have felt about that?"

"She would have been very upset, I guess," I say, frowning.

Kieron nods. "Even more so when she found out that those animals were going to be sold on the black market to the highest bidder for millions."

"That's what was going to happen to them?" I ask, aghast, pulling Silver close to me.

"Yes, according to this article," Kieron says. "Whoever the scientist was who spoke to this journalist, they were *really* brave. Taking on the powerful people behind Magnitude would have been a big risk and a scary prospect."

I glance down at the photograph of Mum with Silver. "You really think the scientist who leaked the story might have been my mum?"

Kieron shrugs. "Maybe."

Placing the photo frame back down on the bedside table, I let out a sigh. "I hope so. Kieron, why don't more people know about this?"

"Well, the project was shut down, the location of the laboratories was abandoned, any trail of paperwork or digital evidence was destroyed. Magnitude buried the scandal before it could be found. After I read the article, I emailed the mystery sender and asked them why they hadn't published it. They replied that the safety of the animals was the priority. I guess whoever wrote the article decided it was safer to keep the existence of these super-animals a secret, so no one would come looking for them. That ended up being more important than exposing the work of Magnitude."

"So, the article was never published and the bravery of the anonymous scientist was wasted," I conclude glumly.

"Not exactly," Kieron counters. "The mere threat of the story being leaked was enough to get the whole project stopped. The animals were freed. Sounds to me like that scientist's behaviour saved them."

I push myself off the bed, and it's my turn to

restlessly pace around, Silver and Kieron watching me intently. This is a LOT of information to process. My mum was involved in a top-secret magical animal project that she potentially might have sabotaged, and somehow one of the animals involved is now my rescue dog, who is being hunted by the other scientists who originally worked alongside my mum.

"This is unbelievable," I say eventually, clutching my pendant in my hand.

"It is a lot to get your head round. We've seen the evidence" – he nods at Silver – "so we know there's truth in it."

"We can't let Callahan get hold of Silver," I say, biting my lip. "I hate that he already has the others. Do you think they're all dogs who can turn into wolves too?"

"No idea. Possibly. Hey, my mum told me that Silver was found sitting on your nan's doorstep, and it was difficult to get him to leave to go to the shelter in the first place. Do you think he was searching for your mum?"

I kneel at the edge of the bed so my face is level with Silver's as he lies across the duvet. As I scratch his neck, he closes his eyes in contented satisfaction.

"You might be right. Poor boy," I say gently. "All this time he was looking for her."

"Yeah, but now he's got *you*," Kieron says. "It's like he finally found his family again."

I smile at the thought, before sitting back cross-legged on the floor. "I can't believe you managed to find all of this information out. Thank you so much, Kieron. I never would have known any of this without you."

"Don't thank me – we need to thank whoever it is who sent me the article."

"And you have no idea who it could be?"

He shakes his head. "I asked who they were, but they never replied. I sent a couple more emails, but that was it. I didn't hear any more from them."

"Did they give you any information about why the animals suddenly transform? What it is that sets off the change? Can they control it?"

"All I got was what was in the article, and there wasn't anything about that in there." He hesitates. "I also can't find anything about … uh … you know, how your eyes change colour when Silver transforms."

"Maybe it happens to whoever is nearest physically to the animal?"

"I considered that, but in the park, I was close to him too, but it was only *your* eyes that changed. I'm going to have to keep looking into that, but I'm worried that only Callahan will have the answer. One thing is for sure: Silver's magic is amazing and rare and precious. And someone like Callahan isn't going to easily give up on getting him back."

"They're going to keep searching for him," I say quietly, my stomach heavy with a feeling of dread. "They have my picture. They knew to look for us in the local park. Do you think we're in a lot of danger?"

"I think we need to be very careful," Kieron says, his eyebrows knitted together. He glances at my sickened expression and quickly adds, "But at least we're in this together. You're not on your own. We won't let him catch Silver. I don't see how he can, anyway, if Silver keeps turning into a wolf like that around him."

"Dean and Chad complained that the other animals weren't in their magical forms when they caught them," I recall. "They must have found a way of sneaking up on them. We need to make sure that we're on alert all the time."

"Yes," Kieron agrees. "And that absolutely no one takes us by surprise."

"Exactly."

"**SURPRISE**!"

We both yelp in horror at Nan's ambush as she bursts into my room, the door suddenly swinging open and banging against the wall. With a thunderous expression, she holds one hand up in the air.

There, pinched between her thumb and forefinger, is one tiny single strand of white dog hair.

*Uh-oh.*

With her other hand, she points accusingly at Silver on the bed. "Luna Wolf," she begins, incensed, "you have a LOT of explaining to do!"

# CHAPTER THIRTEEN

Kieron and I are anxiously perched on the sofa.

Silver is sitting to attention at my feet.

Nan is standing in front of us with her hands on her hips, still wearing her neon-orange headband and leg warmers, despite cancelling on her speed-walking group. After marching us all downstairs, we heard her on the phone explaining that she'd have to miss today's session as she had a "personal issue" to deal with.

Her eyes scan from me across to Kieron. He shivers under her glare, bowing his head and tapping his right foot restlessly. Neither of us dare speak. Even Silver knows who's the boss in this situation:

when he whines impatiently, she shoots him a look and he silences immediately, lying down and resting his head on his paws.

"So…" Nan clears her throat. "Who wants to tell me why there is a dog in my house? Luna? Would you like to start?"

I clasp my hands together. "Um. Well, it's a long story. I'm not sure you'd understand."

She narrows her eyes at me. "*Try me.*"

Kieron shifts in his seat uncomfortably. Silver whimpers.

"OK, so when I started working at the rescue centre, I began to build a bond with Silver—"

"Silver is this dog, I take it," Nan interrupts, gesturing to him, and I nod.

"You may recognize him from when he was found on your doorstep," Kieron chips in, but quickly clams up again under Nan's intense glare.

"Silver and I formed a connection," I continue, taking the heat off Kieron. "He'd never really liked humans before, but he seemed to like me. We became inseparable."

"I see. So, you decided to bring him home despite my strict rules about no pets in the house?" Nan surmises.

"No," I reply quickly. "That's not what happened. Lucy and Dad decided that he could be my dog, but that he'd stay at the rescue centre until Dad and I found a new house. That was the original plan."

"The original plan," Nan repeats. "What changed?"

"The break-in," Kieron says.

"I was too frightened to leave him there after that," I explain. "I'm sure you can understand that, Nan, right? I thought … I thought someone might take him!"

"And then you thought that the best way of going about it was to lie and keep him here behind my back, instead of talking about it with me," Nan says.

"No! Well, sort of no. Kind of, yes." I frown, getting confused. "What I mean is, we'd had many conversations about how you'd NEVER have a dog because they're dirty and stinky, so … so…"

"So, we thought we'd try to prove you wrong,"

Kieron jumps in. "If Silver could live here without you noticing for a couple of days, maybe you'd be more inclined to let him stay. The plan was never to lie to you. Much. Right, Luna?"

"Right. Just a little bit at first, and then we'd tell you the truth. Nan, he's really intelligent and sweet."

"Chimpanzees are intelligent and sweet, Luna, but that does not mean I want one as a houseguest," she points out, ruffled.

"But you haven't even noticed he was here! That's how good he is!"

"Haven't noticed?" She holds up the offending dog hair again. "I found this on the coaster under my cup of tea on the coffee table in this very room!"

"One dog hair, Nan. That's hardly a disaster."

"It starts with one dog hair on a coaster," she huffs, throwing her hand up in the air. "Then it becomes two dog hairs on the kitchen tiles, then it's a clump of dog hair on the sofa, THEN it's dirty paws across the carpet, then mud splattered up the wall by the stairs, and the next thing you know—"

"The dog is wearing your nightie in bed?" Kieron finishes for her, a hint of amusement in his voice.

"Precisely," she confirms, prompting Kieron and I to share a conspiratorial smile when she wasn't looking. "I can understand that the break-in at the shelter gave you a fright; that is to be expected. I can also understand that you were worried to leave your dog there afterwards, especially if you've formed this special connection. But to bring him back here without speaking to me about it? To lie and sneak around behind my back? That is not how we operate, Luna. Your father is going to be very upset when he hears about this, and I'm afraid I'm going to have to tell him."

Before I can respond, we hear the key in the front door and Dad and Lucy come strolling in. They do a double-take when they see us all in the sitting room, and Dad's face falls when he spots Silver at my feet. Lucy grimaces.

"Oh dear," Dad says, putting down a bag of groceries.

"Oh dear indeed, Richard," Nan says, puffing out

253

her chest. "Luna has been keeping this dog in the house without our knowledge."

Dad pauses, and I can see him trying to work out the best course of action. He decides to go with the wrong one.

"WHAT?" he cries in an over-dramatic manner. "I can't believe it! A dog in the house! That's ridiculous! Well, that is … very bad of you, Luna. Really, it is not on."

Nan stares at him. He tries to look angry, but his frown is faltering. Lucy pretends to be very interested in the floor.

After a few moments, Nan rolls her eyes. "Oh, for goodness' sake, how long have you known?" she asks crossly.

"What? I didn't… I had no… I couldn't…" his protesting trails off pathetically, and then he gives up on the act. "I've known a little while. Sorry, Clementine."

"I take it you were also in on this little secret, Lucy?" Nan checks.

She nods. "Sorry, Clementine."

"Sorry, Nan," I add.

"We're all sorry," Kieron says.

Silver lets out a whine.

"I see." Nan sighs, shaking her head. "Well, I'm very disappointed in all of you."

We hang our heads. Nan moves over to the armchair in the corner and sits down.

"I think it would be best to discuss how to move forward from this current predicament over a cup of tea," Nan announces. "Luna, would you mind putting the kettle on?"

Delighted to leave the tense atmosphere of the room, I jump to my feet and rush through to the kitchen, my escape enviously watched by the other participants of the conversation. I'm expecting Silver to follow me, as usual, but he doesn't. Instead, he gets up, stretches, and then plods over to Nan, plonking his bottom down next to her feet.

I'm only out of the room for a few minutes, but by the time I return to the sitting room with the tea, I'm stunned to see Silver's head resting on Nan's knee.

*And she's stroking his head.*

Collecting myself, I don't say anything and set down the tray on the coffee table, before handing a mug of tea over to Nan. She takes it gratefully with both hands and resumes stroking Silver's head after she's set the mug down on the coaster next to her. As I take Dad and Lucy a cup of tea each, I notice that they both look as bewildered by the situation as I do.

"Right, now that we're all present again, let's talk about the best solution," Nan says. "Lucy, do you not think that Silver would be better living happily in the rescue centre until his new home is ready and waiting? I remember Athena talking about how dogs like routine, and I imagine it might not work for him to get used to living here and then move again?"

"Yes, that can certainly be the case for many dogs," Lucy answers. "However, in Silver's case, I would argue that he is a very calm, adaptable dog, who seems most at home in Luna's company, so would probably be most comfortable wherever she is." She pauses, adding, "Although, I must say, Clementine, he looks very happy with you also. There must be something about your family that appeals to this dog. It really is bizarre; he doesn't act this way around anyone else. But you and Luna … well, it's amazing if I'm honest!"

I catch Kieron's eye, and he shoots me a knowing smile. We must both be thinking the same thing: Silver feels connected to my mum through me, her daughter, and Nan, her mother. It makes my heart ache. I wish I could tell Nan everything so she knows how special this dog is and how much he meant to Mum.

But considering how angry she was about finding a dog living under her roof, I'm not sure it's quite the right time to tell her that he is also, on occasion, a wolf.

"Luna has already informed me that Silver is a particularly intelligent dog," Nan says, unfazed by Lucy's remarks about his preference for her. "He clearly understands and respects the hierarchy of this household and is making a play to win me over."

"Is it working?" I ask hopefully.

Nan picks up her mug, takes a sip of tea and then sets it down again, before ignoring my question altogether. "Richard, do you think it's a smart idea to give Luna a pet when she's only twelve years old? Keeping a dog is a big responsibility and isn't a scenario that should be jumped into without any thought."

"I've put a lot of thought into it, I assure you," Dad answers quickly. "Lucy has been keeping me informed on Luna's progress with Silver at the rescue centre, and I've witnessed how well she's done training him. You'll be very proud of her, Clementine, when she shows you all of Silver's tricks. And although I am truly very sorry for allowing her to keep him here secretly, she's been taking him for his daily walks and doing all his feeding and grooming. I haven't helped her at all, except to get you out of the house when she needed to sneak him out," he adds with a chuckle.

Nan's grave expression doesn't budge.

Dad stops laughing. He looks VERY sheepish.

Eventually, he clears his throat. "Anyway, the point to focus on here is that Luna is ready to look after this dog," he says in his most serious and grown-up manner. "I'm certain of that."

"I would agree," Lucy squeaks from behind him.

"Silver was meant to be Luna's dog," Kieron states, sounding a lot more confident than I imagine he feels. "Like I mentioned earlier, he was the dog that arrived on your doorstep. It's like he knew that he had a connection to this family. And he looks a bit like that dog with Luna's mum in the photo by her bed. Don't you think that's strange, Clementine? Fate, or something."

When he's finished, he sits back, having said his piece. Visibly moved by his words, Nan glances down at Silver. He stares devotedly up at her, and I can see she's affected in the same way I was when he first looked at me like that.

As though he's trying to communicate that if you let him, he'll be right here by your side.

Tearing her eyes away from his, Nan continues to stroke Silver's head as we all await her verdict in silence.

"All right," she says eventually. "Silver can stay."

Dad's jaw drops open. Lucy claps a hand over her mouth. Kieron punches the air in celebration.

"Nan," I say, a grin slowly spreading across my face, "are you *serious*?"

"Are you sure, Clementine?" Dad asks.

She nods. "Yes, I'm sure." She looks down at Silver again. "Until you find your new house, you are welcome to stay here, but if I catch you going up the stairs, young man, you'll be in a LOT of trouble." She lifts her head to address the rest of us. "Now, we need to set some ground rules—"

But she doesn't get the chance to finish her sentence.

She's too busy being engulfed in a hug from me, before I'm joined by Kieron, Dad and Lucy. With the four of us piling on top of her, squealing "thank you" in chorus at the top of our lungs, all anyone can hear from her at the bottom of the pile-up is infectious laughter.

# CHAPTER FOURTEEN

I don't notice that anything is wrong until Kieron appears in our garden.

Up until that moment, I'd been having a very good day. Silver has been loving his new-found freedom in the house, enjoying being able to roam about as he pleases with no one to hide from. There are strict rules in place, which we've accepted: he's not allowed upstairs or on any of the furniture, and at meal times, he has to go to his brand-new dog bed and not beg at the table.

Watching Nan in the pet store when we went to buy the dog bed yesterday was very entertaining. She muttered about how spoilt pets were getting these days as she wandered past the accessory stand, which boasted dog bow ties and outfits, but neither Dad nor I missed her eyeing up the neckerchiefs. When the shop assistant asked her if she'd like to put the purple chequered one on Silver to see if it fit, Nan gave her a disapproving look and remarked that if Silver were to have a neckerchief, then it was obvious the blue chequered one would suit him better, or perhaps the golden one to match his eyes.

Dad added the blue one to our basket as he headed towards the check-out with the dog bed under his arm, and Nan told him off for buying something so ridiculous. And yet, when he was wearing his new neckerchief this morning, I caught her positioning it properly on him when she thought I wasn't looking.

It also hasn't gone unnoticed that Silver sometimes will lie at her feet and doze while she's watching her favourite TV shows, and she'll enthusiastically point things out to him about the various characters and their storylines. Even her hourly complaints about the dog hairs have started to wane. And though she insists that he sleeps downstairs in his new bed, rather than allowing him up in my room, I think it's only a matter of time before she'll relent on that one. I've told Silver that we just have to be patient.

He's fit right into our lifestyle here.

So, when Kieron comes sprinting out into the garden where I'm happily playing fetch with Silver, I have no idea that anything has gone wrong. But one look at his face, and I know that something is up. He looks scared and shaken, leaning against the garden door as though he might throw up at any moment.

"Are you OK?" I ask as Silver trots over with the ball and places it in my waiting hand. "Kieron, what's wrong?"

He can't answer me, a mixture of being too upset and too out of breath from having run here. He gestures for me to follow him and quickly darts into the house. Nan is busy doing paperwork at the kitchen table, and as both of us rush past her and up the stairs, she says to let her know if we need anything and reminds Silver, who has followed me in, that he is not to go upstairs if he knows what's good for him.

Sitting on the bottom step, Silver whines loudly, and I promise him I'll be right back down, even though I have no idea how long I'll be. In the meantime, he heads into the kitchen to sit with Nan.

"What's going on?" I ask Kieron as he tells me to shut the door.

"Where's your dad?" he blurts out, his eyes filling with tears.

"At work!"

"Are you sure? Have you spoken to him recently?"

"No, but we don't disturb him at work. He left this morning and he'll be back later. Do you need to talk to him about something? Is Lucy OK?"

Kieron shakes his head and I feel awash with fear.

"Why? What's happened?"

He gets out his phone and brings up his emails. He clicks on the top one in his inbox with the subject: "URGENT: TOP SECRET MAGNITUDE INFORMATION" and opens the attachment. It's a video.

"I just received this," he tells me, holding up the screen so I can see.

He presses play.

At first the video is jolty and shaky, the camera lurching about as whoever's filming has trouble holding it still.

"You have one job, Dean!" says a familiar voice. "All you have to do is hold the camera still and point it at them! It's not hard!"

"It slipped, Chad, it's not my fault!" comes the reply of the man behind the camera. "You were holding it when you were buttering your toast and you've made it all slippery with your greasy fingers."

The shot finally comes into focus. I gasp in horror as Dad and Lucy appear on-screen, both of them gagged and bound, sitting on the ground and backed into the corner of what looks like some kind of large cage.

A figure steps in front of them, and the camera blurs for a moment until it comes back into focus, and we can see who it is.

Callahan.

"As you can see, we have something of yours," he sneers into the lens, gesturing to Dad and Lucy who are squirming behind him and trying to speak, their voices turned into muffled grunts thanks to the cloth twisted and wrapped around their mouths.

"If you want to see your parents again, then I suggest you hand over what belongs to me," Callahan continues. "It's very simple. No one needs to get hurt. The girl, Luna, brings the dog to me – no one else! It has to be Luna Wolf – and in return, I will set these two free. Come this evening to the address provided in the body of this email at eight p.m. Don't be late. Oh, and if you're thinking of calling the police or doing anything clever," he adds, leaning in to the camera and giving a crooked smile, "I wouldn't if I were you. I don't want to harm the hostages, but if you test me, I won't hesitate."

He takes a step back and waits for something to happen.

After a long pause, his eyes dart to above the lens

and he hisses, "Did you zoom in on the hostages?"

"Huh?" Dean replies, the camera jolting as he fumbles with it. "Are you talking to me?"

"Who else would I be talking to?" Callahan seethes, exasperated. "You're the one holding the camera. We talked about this. 'I won't hesitate' was your cue to zoom in on their frightened faces."

"Oh yeah! Right, 'course," Dean replies, the video going blurry again until it comes into focus on someone's forehead.

"That's too close! You're the worst cameraman," Chad scoffs from somewhere behind Dean. "Zoom out a bit."

"Shut up, Chad, I'm trying to concentrate!"

The picture jolts and then comes back into focus on Dad and Lucy.

"There, got a great shot of them," Dean declares, sounding delighted with himself. "What next, boss?"

Callahan sighs, burying his head in his hands. "*Stop the video!*"

"Gotcha, boss."

The video cuts out and Kieron's phone screen goes black.

For a few moments, I stay staring at the blank screen in utter shock.

Then, snapping into action, I grab my phone from my pocket and Kieron watches as I find Dad's name in my contacts and call him. I don't know why. I guess part of me is hoping that the video I just watched somehow isn't real.

It goes straight to voicemail. I lower my phone.

"What are we going to do?" Kieron whispers, terrified.

My mind is racing. I feel sick to my stomach. Poor Dad and Lucy! It takes every inch of willpower I have not to completely freak out and start shouting and screaming. But for Dad's sake, I know I need to keep it together. It's up to me to get them out of this mess.

"I'll go meet them with Silver tonight," I state. "I have to follow their instructions and get Dad and Lucy back."

"But you can't hand Silver over to those

horrible people!"

"I won't," I assure him. "There's no way that they're getting their hands on Silver. I have to work out a way of freeing Dad and Lucy without giving these criminals what they want. I'll have to … I'll have to think up a plan."

"We should call the police," he suggests, anxiously wringing his hands.

"Callahan said not to. We can't let anyone else get involved."

"But we could tell the police the address they've given us. They could break in there and get our parents to safety!"

"Callahan isn't an idiot, Kieron. He'll be keeping a lookout in case we do that. What if he notices that the police are surrounding him? We can't risk him harming Dad and Lucy! Not to mention all the other animals they have captured there."

"They're holding our parents hostage!" Kieron buries his head in his hands. "This doesn't seem real!"

"I know, but it's going to be OK," I tell him, trying

to sound a lot more optimistic than I feel. "I promise. I won't let them win. Somehow, I'll rescue our parents and keep Silver safe and sound. We can't panic, Kieron. We have to be strong for Dad and Lucy."

Groaning, Kieron slumps down on the bed and looks up at me with fresh determination in his eyes.

"Fine. I'm coming with you."

"No. In the video, Callahan said that it needed to be me to bring Silver, no one else. I have to do this alone."

"No, you don't. And anyway, it's my mum in danger too. I want to help," he counters, frowning. "How do you know that Callahan won't have set up a trap for you? How do you know he'll stick to his word and set them free? Even if Silver is in his wolf form, they might be more prepared to catch him this time. They'll be ready for your arrival and, since we're coming to them, they have the upper hand. I won't let you go alone. I'm coming too, and that's final."

The idea of facing Callahan and rescuing our parents all on my own is a bit intimidating, so I'm comforted by Kieron's resolve to come with me.

"OK," I say, nodding. "Thanks."

He sighs. "Remember how when you first arrived in London I was complaining that nothing exciting happens around here? I tempted fate, didn't I?"

"This isn't your fault. If anything, I should be apologizing to you for causing so much trouble," I admit, feeling so guilty and worried I could cry. "Ever since I came along, you've found yourself in all these horrible situations. Trapped in the rescue centre during a break-in, up all night doing research into an old top-secret project during your summer holidays, and now your mum has been kidnapped because an evil scientist wants my dog. I'm so sorry that knowing me has got you into so much trouble, Kieron."

Kieron looks down at his hands. "If I'm honest with you, Luna, although this situation is particularly bad, for all the other ones it's been pretty cool to get into trouble for … a friend. And that's because I haven't had one before. A friend that is."

He shrugs as I stare at him in surprise.

"People at school have never really … got me,"

he adds by way of explanation. "That's why I always help Mum out during the holidays. I didn't exactly have anyone else to hang out with. That party I went to last week? It was a disaster. I'd only been invited because the whole class was going, and no one wanted to talk to me. They started playing with water guns, and no one wanted me on their team. I ended up pretending I had to go home early and snuck out to read my book at a bus stop until it was time for Mum to pick me up, and I walked back to the house to act as though I'd just walked out of the party. Anyway" – he takes a deep breath – "what I'm trying to say is that I like being your friend, no matter how much trouble we get in."

As he says it, I realize that I feel the same. I've felt so alone for a really long time. I've never fit in anywhere and had started to believe that it was better to be invisible because no one enjoyed my company, but I haven't felt that way when I've been hanging out with Kieron. I've been able to be myself around him. It sounds like such a small, simple thing, but it means so much.

I sit down next to him on the bed.

"Same," I say, nudging him with my elbow. "We're in this together. And we're going to save our parents."

"Right. So, where do we start?"

"Funnily enough, the group of evil scientists isn't even our biggest worry."

"What do you mean?"

I grimace. "First things first: I have to somehow sneak out of the house tonight without Nan cottoning on."

Kieron closes his eyes in despair. "Talk about Mission Impossible."

A sick bug.

It's Kieron's idea and, as I told him when he first suggested it, a genius one. Not only would I not want to be disturbed if I had a sick bug, but Nan wouldn't want to come too close, either. We lay the foundations nice and early: after concocting our genius plan, Kieron goes down the stairs, putting on a fantastic act of moaning in pain, clutching his stomach and complaining about feeling ill.

When Nan comes out into the hall to check on him, he tells her to stay away because he doesn't want to pass on the "sick bug that's been going around the rescue centre" and which he's almost certain he has, because suddenly he doesn't feel so good.

"I'll just run home," he croaks, wiping his brow in a martyr-like manner. "I would hate to be sick on your carpets or outside on your petunias. I'd better hurry."

"Wait, I'll take you home," Nan insists, looking concerned. "Let me find my handbag."

"No, no, you must save yourself," he wails, throwing open the front door and backing out of it. "Don't come near me!"

"Let me call Lucy."

"No! No, she's also feeling sick, so best not to disturb her," he says hurriedly. "I promise I'll message when I get home to let you know I'm there. Uh-oh" – he clamps a hand over his mouth and puffs out his cheeks – "I have to go before it's too late!"

He slams the door shut and runs off before Nan has a chance to stop him.

"Poor thing!" she exclaims, going to find her phone. She makes a call, but hangs up quickly. "Lucy's phone is going straight to voicemail. He's right: she must be sleeping it off. I'll message her to let her know that he's on his way home."

"Nan," I whimper from the top of the stairs, bent over double. "My stomach hurts."

"Oh no! Luna, you might have the bug too! Quick, straight to bed and rest. I'll bring you some water."

"I think I'm going to be sick!" I cry, before rushing to lock myself in the upstairs bathroom. I try my best to make a convincing vomiting sound before flushing the toilet a couple of times as I hear her coming up the stairs.

"Are you all right in there?" she asks through the bathroom door.

"Not really," I reply, sounding as weak as possible. "But everyone else who's had this bug at the centre felt better after twenty-four hours, so I think I should sleep it off."

"I'll put a glass of water by your bed, and then I'll start making my pea soup! That cures absolutely everything, trust me."

"I don't really feel like eating, Nan. I think I need to go straight to bed."

"Yes, you rest and then when you're feeling better, you have some of my soup and it will give you all the energy you need to get back on your feet."

"OK, thanks, Nan. But please don't come near me. I really don't want to give this bug to you. You stay downstairs."

"Is there something I can bring you?"

"Nothing, thanks, Nan. I'm going to bed now."

"All right. You tell me if you need anything. I'll start making the soup."

When she's safely back downstairs in the kitchen, I head back into my bedroom and start preparing for tonight, tucking the pillows under my duvet strategically so it looks like I'm sleeping under there if she checks in, and then pulling on my trainers and grabbing Silver's lead and his treats. Kieron said he'd bring a backpack with a torch, his camera and his supplies, so I'm not really sure if there's anything else I can bring that's helpful.

What do you bring with you to face an evil scientist who's holding your dad hostage and trying to steal your magic dog? I look around my room for inspiration, but nothing strikes me. Glancing at the picture of Mum by my bed, I fiddle nervously with the pendant around my neck. I wish she was here to tell me what to do. Everyone tells me she was smart and determined, that once she'd made up her mind about something, she didn't let anyone get in her way. Tonight, I have to try to channel her. I can't let Callahan win.

Even though I still don't know the full story about how involved she was in Magnitude, something tells me that she didn't want Callahan to win, either.

Just before it's time to leave, I pull on my dressing gown and poke my head around my door, calling out to Nan down the stairs.

"Nan? I'm going to go to sleep now!" I yell.

She comes halfway up the stairs and turns to look at me through the banister.

"All right, are you sure I can't bring you anything?"

"No, I just feel really sick, so I'm going to stay in bed for the rest of the night," I tell her, sounding very sorry for myself. "I'll see you in the morning."

"You sleep well. I'll be right here if you need me."

Thanking her, I shut the door and then turn off my bedroom light, perching on the edge of my bed as I listen to her bustling about the kitchen, making the soup. When it's time to leave, I thank my lucky stars that she's decided to put on some music as she cooks, making it much easier to sneak downstairs undetected.

Silver is in his bed in the kitchen, but he lifts his head as he spots me crouching by the banister, signalling for him to come over. Nan is too busy stirring the soup and singing along to the radio to notice him hop out and come hurrying over to me, greeting me with a giant, slobbery lick across the face. I slip the lead over his head and waste no time in leaving the house as Nan belts out a chorus with impressive gusto, masking the sound of the front door shutting behind us.

Silver and I run down the road to the corner where Kieron is waiting, wearing all black from head to toe and clutching the straps of his backpack.

"Ready?" he asks as we reach him, his expression one of steely determination.

"Ready," I confirm, nervous butterflies dancing around my stomach as I think about the rescue mission we're about to attempt. "Let's go."

"Let's," he says, leading the way to the bus stop while he double-checks the map on his phone directing us to Callahan's meeting point. "No going back now."

# CHAPTER FIFTEEN

The address Callahan has given us is a huge warehouse on the outskirts of the city.

At first, when we get off the bus in the middle of nowhere and walk away from the road down a strange, dusty trail lined by overgrown hedgerows near an unused train track, we worry that we're lost or have somehow misread the directions, but then a large grey steel building looms ahead.

Keeping our distance, we stop to duck behind the bushes and scope out our surroundings. Silver growls menacingly as he peers at the warehouse through the leaves, the fur down his back standing on end.

"I recognize this place from the photo next to my bed," I tell Kieron. "Mum is standing right in front of it with Silver. This must have been where Magnitude was based. Silver probably doesn't have good memories of this building."

Pulling his camera out of his bag, Kieron holds it up, adjusts his lens and starts clicking, having informed me on the way here that he was going to document as much as possible so he has proof for when he writes his big story on Magnitude and all the wrongs the corporation has committed.

"It looks abandoned," he remarks, zooming in. "The windows are all boarded up. I don't think this building has been used in years."

"It hasn't. You said they shut down the project."

"Yeah, but you'd think they'd use it for something else, or sell it," he muses. "What's the point in keeping the building empty all these years?"

"Maybe they were holding out until they could start up the project again," I say, swallowing the lump in my throat as I think about the animals stuck in there who they've managed to capture again. "They must have been biding their time."

"There's a man guarding the main door and another standing by a side door," Kieron says, moving the angle of the camera. "They're waiting for you."

"Dean and Chad?"

He lowers his camera and shakes his head. "Nope. We haven't seen these ones before. Callahan has got a few more players on his team than we anticipated."

"Hopefully when I approach with Silver, they'll both come in with me, leaving the doors free for you to sneak in later without being seen."

"I don't think so," Kieron says. "Like you said, Callahan isn't stupid. He knows that I'm involved in this too – he sent the video to my email address, remember? He'll probably guess that I've come with you. I reckon one will stay to keep a lookout."

"How are you going to get past him?" I ask anxiously, feeling like we've failed before we've even begun. "The whole plan relies on the fact that Callahan won't know there are two of us here!"

"Don't worry, I have an idea."

Kieron unzips his backpack and pulls out his Bluetooth speakers and a tennis-ball blaster. I peer into his open bag to see several extendable leads in there as well.

"When you said you were getting supplies for tonight, did you ... get them from the rescue centre?" I ask curiously.

"Yeah, 'course."

I blink at him. "And how exactly are tennis balls and leads going to help us against an evil criminal gang?"

He taps the side of his head. "All you have to do is use a little imagination, Luna. When I went to the centre today to pick up this stuff, I recorded an audio of all the dogs barking excitedly for their food. Once you're inside, I'll be able to distract whichever lookout is left behind by playing that through the speakers. How would you react if you suddenly heard a pack of barking dogs coming from nearby?"

"I suppose I would be a little on edge."

"I'll say." Kieron nods.

"OK, but after he hears the barking dogs … what then?"

"He panics, desperately looking around to see where the sound is coming from, and then" – Kieron holds up the tennis-ball blaster and gives a smouldering look, clearly trying to channel James Bond – "I use the weapon at my disposal."

"You plan on taking him out with … a tennis ball?"

"Don't look so cynical. This blaster shoots out tennis balls with a *lot* of force."

"And the leads?"

He grins mischievously at me. "I'll have to tie his hands and feet up with something."

I can't help but be impressed. "I hope it works."

"It will. I'll follow you in there unseen and will be on hand to help free the hostages. I've brought some bolt cutters too, so I can hopefully cut through any padlocks – it looked like they had Mum and Richard in some kind of cage. It's a foolproof plan," he claims with a shrug. "What's *your* plan for once you're in there?"

"I don't want to say."

"Come on. Tell me. I filled you in on mine, even though it sounds stupid. We're in this together, remember?"

I sigh, glancing down at Silver, who still has his cautious eyes fixed on the warehouse. "OK. Um … well … I was going to pretend that I'm cooperating so Callahan's guard is down, walk in there and hope that Silver turns into a wolf."

Kieron watches me apprehensively.

"And?" he prompts when I don't say anything else.

"That's it."

"*That's it?*" He looks stunned. "Your plan is to stroll into the lion's den and simply HOPE that Silver turns into a wolf? That's not a plan!"

"Well, I didn't have much time to prepare!"

"I had the same amount of time and managed to create a plan AND weaponize!"

"With dog toys," I point out defensively.

"*Effective* dog toys," Kieron corrects. "Luna, this

is serious."

"I'm going to have to improvise! I don't have any idea what to expect in there. The only way Callahan is going to let me near our parents is if he thinks that I'm going along with the swap. Once I'm in, I'll work out how to free Dad and Lucy."

"Lucky for you, I brought spares. Here, take this." Kieron holds out another tennis-ball blaster. "Just in case."

"They'll take it from me the minute I walk in. I'm meant to look like I'm coming in peace, remember? Don't worry, Kieron, I'll be OK. I've got Silver. He'll look after me. Plus, you're my secret weapon – Callahan won't know you're here. The element of surprise is always a strong one."

Unconvinced, Kieron sighs, lowering the spare tennis-ball blaster.

I check the time on my phone.

"It's time to go," I declare. "You stay here and wait a bit before you put your plan into action. Once you're in the building, try to remain hidden as long as you can, and hopefully Silver and I will find a way of distracting Callahan and his men so you can free Dad and Lucy without them noticing."

"If only we knew how to turn Silver into a wolf on command," Kieron says regretfully. "Sending you both in there unarmed and leaving his transformation to chance seems risky."

"The only times he's changed has been around Callahan," I remind him. "That can't be a coincidence. We'll be OK, Kieron. Have a little faith."

Silver gives his leg a comforting nudge with his nose, making him jump. Kieron laughs with relief when he realizes it's just Silver and gives him a pat on the head.

"You look after Luna," he instructs. "Be a good dog. I mean … be a good *wolf*."

Silver licks his hand.

"We'll see you in there," I say, before taking a deep breath, gripping Silver's lead tightly and leaving Kieron crouched behind the hedge as I straighten and continue down the path towards the warehouse.

The man guarding the main door spots me approaching, and I see him put a finger to his earpiece and say something, prompting the other guy by the side door to walk around to join him in greeting me.

"We've got this," I mutter under my breath, glancing down at Silver.

He looks up at me and growls. I nod back at him.

"Luna Wolf," one of the men bellows as I get closer. "Follow me."

Turning his back to me, he pushes open the door and holds it open so I can follow him in. His colleague watches me pass from behind his sunglasses, remaining outside to take over guarding the building as Kieron suspected.

As I take my first steps into the warehouse, my heart is thudding so hard against my chest, I can hear it ringing in my ears. I hope I look a lot more cool and confident than I feel. I scan the large room we've entered, which looks like an old reception area. There's a long desk in the middle which must once have been a gleaming silver, but is now dusty and faded, and the four chairs at it are draped in white sheets. The wall behind the desk is a bright white and looks as though it used to have a giant emblem nailed in the centre of it, but whatever it was has been removed, and all that's been left behind are the punched holes in the wall from the fixings that held it in place.

The bodyguard leads me around to the silver doors behind the desk, punching a code into the panel by the side of them. The light goes green, and there's a loud buzz as we're granted access. We walk in silence down a cold, clinical corridor, the brightness of the strip lights down the ceiling on the white walls causing me to squint. I'm envious of the guard's sunglasses.

Silver lets out a whine as we pass the row of doors leading off the corridors and when I stop to look into one, it looks like the science laboratory at my old school, but as though none of the students had bothered to clean up after themselves. Bits of old apparatus are lying around, beakers and flasks lying on their sides, petri dishes stacked by sinks, dusty microscopes untouched for years. The blackboards have been wiped, though, and there are no computers, notes or files anywhere.

"Oi!"

I jump as the guard barks at me from the end of the corridor where he's waiting. Gulping, I make my way towards him with Silver. The guard turns and puts in the code again for this next set of doors. Stepping through, he blocks my way as he announces our presence to the room.

"The girl and the dog are here."

"Good," I hear Callahan say. "Show them in."

The guard steps back and I nervously shuffle in past him. This room is huge and looks like it was once the main laboratory, right in the middle of the warehouse. There are a number of workstations complete with their own sinks dotted around the room, hosting a similar set of abandoned apparatus like in the rooms we've passed, and beyond them a set of giant cages. The door closes behind us, the sound of it clunking shut echoing across the vast space.

Callahan is standing ahead of me in the middle of the room. A security team of many guards, including Dean and Chad, are dotted around the edge.

"Luna, welcome!" Callahan announces, throwing out his arms. "Please, come closer. We don't want to be shouting at one another. I would hate for you to strain your voice."

"It's OK, Silver," I whisper, doing my best to comfort him and reassure myself at the same time. "I won't let them take you."

We walk across the squeaky floor, watched in silence by all the security guards.

"That's better," Callahan says when we get within a few metres. "Thank you for coming to meet me. I must apologize for the dramatic nature of the video, but, since your little friend has been poking his nose in some places it shouldn't be, I thought it was the best way to get his attention."

"Where are my dad and Lucy?" I demand to know, the wobble in my voice giving away my nerves.

"They're right here," he says, stepping to his right

and gesturing behind him.

My blood turns to ice as I see my dad tied up next to Lucy in the cage, looking at me with wide, desperate eyes and trying to say something to me that's all muffled behind the gags. I think he's saying "*run*".

They're not alone in the cage. There are four animals stuck with them behind the bars: an orange tabby cat curled up in the corner, a white ferret scurrying around the floor, a sparrow flitting about above their heads and, in a glass hutch by their feet, a small green gecko.

"Let them go!" I yell, any fear wiped away by a swell of anger. "Let all of them go!"

Callahan sniggers. "No deal. However, I am willing to set your dad and his partner free, but you know the price for that one."

Silver barks at him, straining at the lead and causing Callahan to jump with fright before he collects himself.

"Hand over the dog," he demands, clicking his fingers at Chad and pointing at a dog-catcher pole that's propped up against one of the cages.

"How do I know you'll let them go?" I ask angrily. "Why should I trust you?"

Callahan sneers, gesturing to the guards standing by around the room.

"I'm not sure you have a choice."

I have to stall him. Right now, Kieron could have made his way into the building, or he could have been captured, but either way I need to buy time. I had hoped that Silver might have turned into a wolf by now, but despite Callahan's presence, he's still a dog.

"This place is where Magnitude was based, right?" I call out.

"That's right." He glances around the room wistfully, shoving his hands in his pockets. "This is where we did some of our greatest work, an example of which you have on the end of that lead. We were going to change the world. I was going to be rich beyond my wildest dreams."

"But then the project was stopped."

His expression darkens. "It was sabotaged. I lost

everything. But then, two years ago, it all changed. We realized that we could start our work again and create a host of super-animals. Two years ago, a single picture gave us hope again."

"You saw a picture of Silver?" I ask, confused. I could have sworn he didn't show up on Nan's doorstep until about a year ago so the photo of him wouldn't have been up on the rescue centre website *two* years ago.

Callahan throws his head back and roars with laughter.

"You have no idea, do you? No clue whatsoever! You think the *animals* are the key to Magnitude? No! They are our prototypes. Do you know how much that dog is worth? Thousands. Maybe even millions."

"He's *priceless*," I state, narrowing my eyes at him, the anger bubbling through me.

Callahan snorts. "The animals are nothing compared to the magic."

"What are you talking about?"

"The magical source that worked for your mother," he says simply, watching me. "Athena Wolf was a brilliant scientist, Luna. Naive, infuriating and righteous, yes. But also brilliant. With the magic she was able to wield using the energy source Magnitude discovered, we could create any super-animal we liked. When the project was shut down because of her lack of ambition and skewed sense of right and wrong, I thought it was lost for ever."

"I don't understand."

"She destroyed it!" Callahan bellows. "That's what we were led to believe. She destroyed the magic so that no one could use it ever again. And then, two years ago, we saw a picture in a local Wiltshire newspaper. An announcement of Athena's Meadow being finished, a field named in honour of the late scientist, Athena Wolf."

"What about it?"

"They printed a photo of her and her daughter that had been taken before she died a few years earlier."

I swallow the lump in my throat. "So?"

"So," he says slowly, "in the photo, she was wearing a necklace with a jagged blue pendant. I recognized it immediately. It was a cut from the stone that contained the magical source. She may have destroyed most of it. But, it turns out, she didn't destroy it all."

I stare at him, trying to process what he's saying.

"Why do you think I demanded that it be specifically *you* who brought the dog to us tonight?" Callahan asks, his lips twisting into a thin smile. "Why do you think I took the picture of *you* that was up on the wall of that rescue centre? Why did I need Dean and Chad to capture *both* of you in the park, not just the dog? Didn't you wonder why? It's because I don't just want the dog back, Luna. I want the magic back too."

He takes a step towards me, his eyes glinting in the light as he continues.

"The magic that's been hanging around your neck all this time."

# CHAPTER SIXTEEN

Mum's necklace is magical.

My first thought is that he's lying, that it's too ridiculous to be true. But then, when I really think about it, answers to a lot of questions start falling into place. If Silver's magic is linked to the necklace, then that's why his transformation into a wolf only began happening when I met him. That must have been what drew him to me above anyone else and why my eyes turn golden when he transforms: the magic stone hanging around my neck, the source of his powers. Every time that Silver turned into a wolf, it was when I was touching him. The magic of the necklace ran through me and connected us.

That's why I got that strange feeling.

As my brain desperately tries to process this information, my hand automatically flies to the pendant, and Callahan watches me, cackling.

"You didn't think that Silver's magic had anything to do with you personally, did you? Perhaps you thought you were special," he sneers, shaking his head. "It is simply by chance that that necklace ended up with you. Your mother had no right  to destroy the rest of the source, and she had no right to take what remained. So, hand it over, along with the dog, and then I'll happily let you and your family go. Athena got all the glory last time, but now it's my turn to wield that magic at last."

A movement at the back of the room momentarily distracts me.

Looking past Callahan, I watch as Kieron enters with the security guard that had been left outside to man the door. The guard has his hands tied behind his back with an extendable lead and his ankles tied together with another, having to shuffle forward very carefully so as not to fall over. Kieron is holding the tennis-ball blaster to his head. The guard has round red marks on his forehead, his left cheek and a couple down both arms – the kind of red mark that's left when you're struck with great force by a tennis ball. With the threat of the tennis-ball blaster, Kieron's used him to get the code to the doors.

I regret making fun of his "weapons" now.

I get a rush of hope as they sneak in undetected by any of the other guards, all of whom are watching Callahan, Silver and me with great interest. I have to keep them distracted. Noticing me looking over his shoulder, Callahan makes to turn round, but I stop him by blurting out a question.

"Why would my mum go into business with someone like you? I don't believe that you ever had the talent to work alongside her on this magic!"

"How dare you?" Callahan spits, his face reddening with fury. "I have always been just as talented and brilliant as Athena! We were both hired at the same time by Magnitude. But she was so controlling that she wouldn't let anyone else attempt the magic with the animals. It just *had* to be her."

"She didn't trust you," I say proudly. "That's why she wouldn't let you near it."

"She could see that I was more ambitious than she was. If she'd had half my vision, then together we could have changed the world. But she held me back. In the end, she nearly ruined me! Setting the animals free, speaking to that journalist, telling him what we were working on here and almost burying Magnitude for ever!"

"So, it *was* Mum who leaked the story," I say, awash with relief. "She thought you were developing the magic to help animals, but you tricked her."

"It was unbelievably naive of her," he sighs. "Honestly, for someone so bright, Athena really let herself down there. She didn't have any inkling of what she was helping us to develop. She really thought we wanted to advance animal healthcare and medicine."

"She loved these animals," I say, looking down at Silver. "She wanted to help them."

Callahan lifts his eyes to the ceiling. "Yes, it was all very sweet. But unfortunately, when it comes to business, she didn't quite have the initiative or ambition that the rest of us had. If only she could have seen sense."

Kieron has, by now, crept up along the cages to the one where Dad, Lucy and the animals are being held. Keeping the tennis-ball blaster pointed at the guard's head, he carefully places his bag down to reach inside for the bolt cutters. Dad and Lucy are watching him tensely.

"You used Mum and her research," I cry out to Callahan, hoping my dramatics will keep him focused on me and that he'll remain with his back to the cage. "You twisted her work into something evil!"

"A crude way of putting it, but yes, that was the plan. Only, one day she found out what our plans were," he grumbles.

"She put a stop to all of it."

He folds his arms. "Yes, she did. But only for a few years. As soon as we saw the necklace in the picture and knew there was hope, we started trying to track down the animals again. A year into our search and we'd got nowhere. And then would you believe it? Another newspaper article led us right to them! A journalist named Rex Robinson had broken his foot and it made the local news when the paramedics arrived to find a host of animals at his house. The very animals we'd lost. But one got away…"

"Silver."

"We know him as Animal Number Five. He didn't have a name when he was here. Except for when your mother talked about him."

"Mum gave him a name? What was it?" I ask eagerly.

"How should I know?" he says, disgusted. "I couldn't care less what she called the stupid mutt. As long as he could transform into a wolf, what did his name matter? I only had to put on a pretence around *her* that I cared one jot about him."

"But she saw through you in the end."

"Eventually," he says wearily. "She helped them escape, told the story, tried to ruin the good name of Magnitude. But all her efforts have come to nothing. The project was temporarily paused, but here we are again with the animals and the magic." Callahan smirks and holds out his hand. "Now, give me the necklace," he says.

"Who is the person financing Magnitude?" I ask, watching Kieron carefully reach the bolt cutters out to the padlock on the cage. "Who is the person behind all of this?"

"Enough chit-chat!" Callahan barks. "I said *give me the necklace*. Or I'll have to take it from you!"

The bolt cutters make contact with the padlock and the chain rattles.

"HE'S HELPING THEM ESCAPE!" yells the guard that Kieron's holding hostage, suddenly deciding to risk being hit in the head by a tennis ball.

Callahan spins around. Kieron freezes.

"I told you to be quiet, or else!" Kieron tells the guard in exasperation, before pressing a button to set off the blaster. The tennis ball comes flying out, smacking the guard across the cheek and causing him to yowl in pain before crumpling to the ground.

"GET HIM!" Callahan yells.

But before anyone can move, a dazzling blue light fills the space. I've already reached down to put my hand on Silver's head and it's as though, in that moment, I instinctively know how to cause the magic to flow through me to him. The last few times, the magic must have worked because it knew we were in danger, but this time, I feel more in control of it, commanding it to work without having to say a word.

The warmth envelops me, and Silver transforms at my touch, letting out an electrifying howl that echoes through the laboratory as he becomes a fierce, giant, majestic wolf.

A collective gasp ripples through the room. The guards look terrified. Dad's eyes are bulging out of his head. Lucy looks as though she might faint.

Kieron is too busy loading both tennis-ball blasters to pay any attention.

Callahan looks on Silver in both awe and fear, edging away backwards with his hands out in front of him. Glancing at me, a flash of recognition crosses his features. As he continues to back away slowly, trying not to make any sudden movements, he addresses the security team, who have been too stunned to move.

"Get the girl," he instructs, pointing a finger at me. "You see her eyes? She's the one in control! Without her, the wolf's magic won't work. Capture her and remove that necklace."

Finishing his sentence, he spins around and races to the nearest empty cage, shutting himself inside and watching the rest of the action from behind the safety of its bars.

Crouched in preparation next to me, Silver's tail swishes from side to side.

*Not yet*, I tell him without saying a word.

He lets out a low, threatening growl, his golden eyes scanning the roughly formed semicircle of guards who are building up the courage to come closer, all of them hoping another will make the first move. Silver snaps his jaws at them in warning.

"You *idiots*!" Callahan seethes from his cage, resting his forehead against the bars. "Why do you think I armed you with tranquilizers? For the WOLF, remember? You're prepared for this! Honestly, am I the only one in this room with a BRAIN?"

The men brighten at this prompt, remembering the tranquilizer guns in their holsters. As they reach for them, I will Silver to follow my instruction.

*Behind here!*

Quick as a flash, we both take shelter behind one of the workstations nearby, ducking behind it just in time as tranquilizer darts shower over our heads. The guard who had escorted us into the building in the first place has been lingering behind us all this time, and now he nervously approaches where we're crouching from that vantage point, aiming his tranquilizer gun down towards us with trembling hands.

I will Silver to leap into action, and he doesn't hesitate. Petrified, the guard clumsily pulls the trigger, but Silver deftly dodges the dart and it hits a beaker sitting on top of the workstation, sending it toppling over the other side where it smashes on the ground. Silver bounds at him, and the guard lets out a scream as he's sent flying backwards, landing with a thud and pinned to the floor by Silver's enormous paws.

Lying in a daze on the flat of his back, the guard takes one look up into the jaws of the wolf looming over him and promptly faints.

Silver returns to my side.

*Good boy*, I think, smiling at him.

There's a pause in proceedings as the rest of the security guards bear witness to Silver's swift and easy overpowering of one of their team who dared to get too close.

"What do you think you're doing? What do I pay you for?" Callahan cries out. "Get them! Get them!"

As the waves of darts resume, and we duck lower, I can sense Silver's restlessness to attack.

*Wait it out*, I think, and sure enough, soon we hear empty clicks and the onslaught of darts comes to a stop.

"We're out of tranquilizer darts!" Dean yells, his voice high-pitched with fear.

"What did you go and say that for?" Chad scolds him furiously. "Now they know you fool!"

"They would have found out anyway when all the darts stopped coming at them, Chad," Dean argues. "Duh!"

"SHUT UP AND GET THEM!" Callahan bellows.

"I'll go for the boy. You lot get the girl and the wolf," Chad instructs.

"That doesn't seem fair," Dean huffs. "How come we have to take on the giant, scary super-animal, whereas you—"

*Now*, I nod to Silver.

I blink and he's gone. Hearing a host of curdled cries, I peer over the edge of the workstation to see guards scarpering in all directions as Silver prowls towards them, barking and baring his fangs. He's already knocked one guard over, who is now scrambling away towards the door on his hands and knees, squealing, "I didn't sign up for this!" and I'm just in time to see him pounce on another, managing to grip the material of the guard's trousers in his jaws and ripping it away to reveal green dinosaur pants beneath. With a horrified screech, the guard's hands fly to his bottom on show, and he sprints away, exiting the room.

Spitting out the trouser cloth, Silver suddenly jerks his head back towards me, his eyes flashing with alarm.

*Watch out*, he communicates.

His warning alerts me to Dean, who has skirted around the workstation and is creeping forward with his arms outstretched, ready to grab me. Glancing around for inspiration, I grab an old Bunsen burner and lob it at him. It hurtles through the air and drops with a loud clunk on his foot.

He yowls with pain, hopping about on his other foot

before losing his balance and toppling over, rolling back and forth, clutching his injured foot in his hands. I turn back to Silver, and he nods to me in satisfaction.

*Nice shot,* he says.

Having scared off the majority of the guards, Silver rounds on the few remaining while Kieron is keeping Chad at bay by relentlessly pelting him with tennis balls.

"OOF! OUCH! YIKES! OW! STOP! EEK! ARGH!" Chad cries, his arms flying around as he attempts to defend himself.

I gasp as Kieron runs out of ammo and Chad takes the opportunity to grab him.

"Get off me," Kieron yells, fighting back as Chad takes him by the scruff of his neck, but he is easily overpowered. Having forced Kieron's arms behind his back, Chad reaches for a key in his pocket and unlocks the cage that Dad and Lucy are in, before throwing Kieron in to join them. Distracted by Kieron's capture, I don't heed Silver's warning until it's too late.

*Behind you!*

I feel strong arms clasp around me and lock me in. Silver's already running back towards me, crossing the room with unhindered speed in his vast strides, but it's too late. The necklace is ripped from my neck and chucked away from me. I watch helplessly as it skitters across the floor.

The laboratory is filled with a blinding blue light and when it wanes, Silver is back in his dog form, barking wildly as he comes running to my aid. Just because he's not a wolf doesn't mean he's lost any courage or his protective nature, and with a ferocious snarl, he pounces towards my captor, wrapping his jaws around his leg.

From his anguished scream, I realize it's Dean who has caught me. He must have got up without me noticing and I curse myself for not keeping an eye on him.

"HELP!" Dean shrieks, loosening his grip as he desperately tries to shake Silver off. "He's got me! He's got me!"

Breaking free from his arms, I rush towards the necklace.

But Callahan is quicker.

As soon as the magic vanished, he'd made his move, dashing from the cage. He sweeps the pendant up in his fingers before I can reach it and holds it up victoriously.

"At last!" he roars.

Grabbing the dog-catcher pole, Chad has managed to make his way to help Dean, and Silver yelps and whines as the hoop is thrown around his neck, trapping him.

"NO!" I cry, turning back to help him. "Let him go!"

"Someone get her!" Chad growls, wrestling with the pole as Silver shakes his head, frantically trying to get free.

Cornered by two guards, one of them pins my hands behind my back and my knees buckle as I watch Silver squirming hopelessly.

"Please don't hurt him!" I beg Chad.

"We should kill him if you ask me," Dean says,

snivelling as he inspects his ripped trousers and the teeth marks in his calves. "That stinky mutt almost took my leg off!"

"Stop blubbering, Dean," Chad sneers. "It was only a little nip."

"Oh yeah? I'd like him to give you a 'little nip' and see how you like it," Dean grunts.

"Can you two please stop bickering for ONE MINUTE?" Callahan cries, still holding the necklace up aloft, like a trophy. "You," – he addresses the guard holding me – "put her in the cage with the others. Chad, bring the dog to me."

"Don't touch him!" I yell at Callahan as I'm dragged towards the cages.

Callahan cackles with delight as he watches me being thrown helplessly behind the bars. Kieron has already untied Dad and Lucy, and I fall into Dad's arms as the cage door is shut with a loud clang.

"Are you OK, Luna?" Dad asks, holding me tight.

I nod against his chest. "I'm so sorry, Dad."

"Why are you sorry?" He pulls away to look me

in the eye. "I've never been so proud of you! I can't believe I have such a brave daughter!"

"This is all my fault," I sob as Lucy comes to put her arm around me too, and I find myself nestling against her. "I'm so sorry I got you all into this."

"This *isn't* your fault!" Lucy insists, squeezing me, before glaring at Callahan and raising her voice so it echoes through the room. "These are the horrible actions of a delusional, power-hungry man who will NEVER get away with it!"

"I've already won," Callahan sneers at her, swinging the pendant from side to side, before turning to Chad who is still attempting to grapple with Silver. "Stop messing around and get that dog over here *now*!"

Flooded with guilt and misery, I've never felt so down in all my life, and it's as though the animals in the cage with us can sense that somehow: the sparrow flits down to land on my shoulder, and the ferret patters across the floor to my feet, climbing up my leg and making his way into my arms, where he

curls up, his red eyes blinking up at me. The orange tabby cat comes to sit at my feet, meowing and rubbing her head against my shin.

"Whoa, that's weird," Kieron notes as the others seem equally startled at their behaviour. "Even the gecko is trying to get to you, Luna."

Seeing that he's right and the gecko is clambering against the glass, I bend down to open his hutch, safely cradling the ferret with my other arm, and the gecko crawls out into the palm of my hand.

"It's like they know you," Lucy says in wonder.

"Maybe they do," Dad insists softly. "They can

sense your mother through you, Luna, I'm sure of it."

And as I look into the eyes of these beautiful animals, whom my mum once loved and devoted herself to, I know he's right.

"Oh, PLEASE!" Callahan guffaws. "Enough with this pathetic drivel! Animals can't sense *anything*. They're stupid animals! They can't tell who's who."

"You're wrong," I tell him through gritted teeth. "They know *exactly* who you are."

"And what I am is the victor," he declares, his eyes flashing at me triumphantly as Chad finally reaches him with Silver. "You've lost, Luna Wolf, and your mum has finally lost too. Now it's my turn to be in control. I have the magic back. I have the power! At my touch, this brutish wolf is mine and will do whatever I bid!"

We all watch on in horror as Callahan clasps the necklace around his neck.

With dramatic flair, he raises his hand high into the air before lowering it on to Silver's back and …

… nothing happens.

# CHAPTER SEVENTEEN

*Nothing happens.*

There's no blue light. Silver doesn't change.

Callahan frowns, then shakes his head and confidently tries again.

Lifting his hand, he presses it down on to Silver's fur.

Nothing.

Callahan starts to panic, his eyes darting about as he makes yet another attempt, moving his hand up and down Silver's back as though the placement might have something to do with it.

"*Come on!*" he seethes, using his free hand to shake the pendant. "Why isn't this working?"

"What's going on, boss?" Chad asks, doing his best to keep control of Silver, who is turning his head to snap at Callahan every time he touches him. "Is it broken?"

"It can't break, you twit!" Callahan bellows, losing his temper. "It's magical!"

The guards share concerned glances as Callahan continues to pat Silver across the back, his face growing redder and redder. Eventually he stops, breathing heavily, staring in dismay at my dog, who snarls back at him.

"This can't be," he whispers. "It *has* to work. It has to. Something must be wrong. Something must have—"

He stops abruptly, turning and marching over to me with a thunderous expression.

"You tampered with it!" he accuses. "What did you do? TELL ME!"

"I didn't do anything. I didn't even know what it was until now!"

"Then why isn't it working?" he cries.

"But it did work for her," Chad points out,

nodding to me. "We all saw it work for her. This dog turned into a wolf right in front of our eyes."

Callahan rounds on him. "*I know that.*"

Chad cowers, dropping his eyes to the floor.

"This isn't possible," Callahan mutters, looking about him desperately for answers. The room waits in silence. He moves back to Silver again, and ordering Chad to keep him steady, he inhales deeply through his nose, his nostrils flaring, and for a final time, puts his hand on the dog's back.

Silver does not transform.

"Get over here," Callahan barks at Dean, who's been watching the spectacle from near our cage. "You try."

He hands Dean the necklace and taps his foot impatiently as Dean fiddles with the chain, putting it on. Receiving a go-ahead nod from Callahan, Dean rubs his hands together in hope and then reaches out to touch Silver's back.

Once more, nothing happens.

Dean looks disappointed. Chad seems relieved,

likely having envisioned how unbearable his colleague would be if it had turned out he could wield magic. Callahan tells Dean to take the necklace off, before asking another guard to give it a go. But it's the same story. There's no magic. Silver remains a dog.

"WHY AREN'T YOU WORKING?" Callahan screeches at the necklace as it dangles from his fingers. "It's not possible! It worked all those years ago! Athena would show me what she did for the animals to change, I saw it with my own eyes. I saw it in the park! I've seen it again today! This dog should be turning into a wolf! Unless … unless…"

Losing himself in his thoughts, he trails off, pacing back and forth. He stops and slowly brings his eyes up to meet mine.

"Unless the magic doesn't work for everyone," Dad suddenly announces, causing all of us to turn to him. He's wearing an expression of deep satisfaction and pride. "It worked for Athena and now it's working for Luna. I think the answer is obvious: you're not worthy of this magic, Callahan."

"It's not a question of being worthy!" Callahan disputes, but he doesn't look so sure.

"The magic *chose* Athena," Lucy says, her eyebrows knitting together as she begins to understand. "And it's chosen her successor. Luna, the magic has chosen you!"

"Luna," Kieron begins ecstatically, "you're like … like an Animal Wizard or something!"

"Animal Wizard?! Don't be ABSURD!" Callahan rages, throwing his hands up. "That can't be … that's not what… YOU'RE WRONG!"

"The animals are responding to her," Kieron points out. "Weren't you just saying that they were stupid, Callahan? Seems to me they've known a lot more than you this whole time. The magic has picked a side – and it's not yours."

Flabbergasted, Callahan lets Kieron's words sink in. I'm as stunned as everyone else that the magic isn't working for him, but I couldn't be happier that Callahan's plan is crumbling before his eyes.

"I can't believe this," Callahan croaks eventually. "This can't be happening."

"It's happening all right," Kieron says smugly. "You're not the victor after all. Athena must have known you would never be worthy. She was never going to let Magnitude win."

Callahan's eyes flash with anger and his jaw clenches.

"Your family have ruined everything," he seethes. "You will pay for this. I am going to destroy everything that you hold dear! I will never rest until I—"

**_CLANG!_**

Suddenly, Callahan is hit around the back of the head by what looks like a frying pan. He falls flat on his face mid-sentence, knocked unconscious. And the person standing behind him wielding the frying pan is none other than—

"NAN!" I gasp as she steps over Callahan and bends down to pick up the necklace that came loose from his fingers as he fell.

"What a rude young man!" she comments, tutting at Callahan sprawled on the floor. "No one threatens my family, thank you very much."

"Nan, what are you doing here?" I ask, beaming at her from the cage.

"You thought you could sneak out of the house without my knowledge, did you?" she scolds, waggling her finger at me. "Pillows under the duvet – what do you take me for, a fool? I followed you here. It took me a long time to work out the codes to get through those doors, but I got the combination in the end. You are in big trouble, Luna Wolf. As soon as you're out of that cage, we are going to have a long chat about your habit of sneaking around behind my back."

I grimace. "Sorry, Nan, but I had to—"

"Rescue your father and Lucy? No excuse," she says crossly, stomping over to the cage. "We'll talk about this later, but for now: here. I believe this belongs to you."

She passes the necklace through the bars into my hand.

"Who has the key to this cage?" she demands to know from the guards. "Come on! Speak up! Who?"

Dean nervously points at Chad. "He does! Not me!"

"You are such a tattle-tale, Dean!" Chad hisses, the colour draining from his face as he sees Nan fix him with one of her famous glares. "N-not just me! A few of us have one. But we're not handing it over! And that's f-final. You don't scare us."

"Is that right?" Nan says, holding up the frying pan. Chad gulps.

Worried about the trouble that Nan is about to get herself into, Dad quickly turns to me and encourages me to put on the necklace, helping me with the clasp.

"Make your mum proud," he says simply, stepping back.

Lucy and Kieron move to stand next to him, all three of them smiling. Bolstered by their belief in me, I take a deep breath and check the animals are ready. They're all looking at me expectantly, as though they've been waiting for this for a while now.

Shutting out everything else around me and concentrating on what the necklace can do, I instantly start to feel different – a warm, wonderful swell of sparkling magic tingles up through my whole body.

The room is filled with a shimmering blue light.

There is no longer a sparrow on my shoulder. In its place, a striking eagle takes flight into the air, spreading her wings and soaring in a circle over our heads.

Where a tabby cat sat by my feet, there is now a huge tiger letting out a deep roar.

Instead of a gecko sitting in my palm, a crocodile crawls across the floor, snapping his jaws.

And the white ferret that was comfortably cradled in the crook of my arm has transformed into an enormous polar bear.

Dad, Lucy and Kieron have flattened themselves against the side of the cage.

"I now understand why these cages were designed to be so big," Kieron squeaks, his eyes as wide as saucers. "They … they won't hurt us, will they, Luna?"

"No," I say calmly, feeling connected to each of these creatures. "They won't."

I give the polar bear a sharp nod and, understanding my instruction, he takes a couple of steps back for a run-up and then charges at the cage door, ramming against it and breaking the flimsy chain that had held it shut. The door swings open.

"Ah," Nan says, lowering her frying pan just as she reaches Chad, "well, that solves that problem. I don't think I'll be needing the key after all."

The guards are standing frozen to the spot, their jaws hanging open.

I grin at my squad of animals, gesturing to the open door. "After you," I offer.

The polar bear heads out, followed by the prowling tiger and the snapping crocodile, while the eagle swoops over their heads. The tiger lets out an almighty roar as they stand in a line to face the guards.

"RUUUUUUUUUN!" Chad yells at the top of his lungs, dropping the dog-catcher pole and sprinting away at full speed.

The guards don't need telling twice. Screaming wildly, all of the security guards turn on their heels and scarper towards the exit, pushing each other out of the way to get through the doors first, the animals hot on their heels, the eagle swooping menacingly over their heads.

"Wait for me, Chad! Wait for me!" Dean cries, hobbling at the back of the crowd thanks to his injured leg. He glances over his shoulder to see the polar bear stand on its hind legs and loom over him, swiping through the air at Dean's head with his sharp claws.

"AAAARGHHHH!" Dean shrieks, throwing himself at the doors and crashing through them.

The polar bear lowers himself and lets out a mocking snort.

The animals knew I didn't want them to actually hurt anyone; they were just on a mission to scare them.

"They're going to get away," Kieron points out,

unable to hide his disappointment as we file out of the cage and watch the doors at the other end of the room swing closed behind Dean. "Those people should be behind bars."

"Oh, don't you worry about that," Nan assures him, going over to Silver to free his neck from the hoop of the dog-catcher pole. "The police are waiting for them outside. I called them when I arrived."

"Well done, Clementine," Lucy says, impressed. "That was smart thinking."

"Silver!" I call out, running towards him as he's released.

My dog comes racing into my arms, and as I fall to my knees to hug him, there's another flash of blue light and I'm suddenly kneeling on the floor with my arms around the neck of a wolf. He nuzzles his snout against my head. He's warm and safe. My heart feels like it might burst with relief and happiness to be reunited with him.

Having accomplished their task of getting rid of the guards, the animals return to gather around us.

Even though they know they won't be hurt, Lucy, Dad and Kieron still look a little on edge in the company of a polar bear, tiger, wolf, crocodile and eagle.

Nan doesn't seem all that bothered to be in their presence. In fact, for a moment I think she might be about to tell off the eagle for causing a mess and knocking over a couple of beakers when she comes in to land on a workstation.

"This is incredible," Dad says, marvelling at the animals. "I can't believe Athena never told me about any of this. She always said she was working on something that would blow my mind, but *this*? It's really quite … something."

"It was a top-secret project," Kieron reasons. "No one but those working on it would have been allowed to know. Athena knew how precious the magic was. That's why she couldn't bear to see it in the wrong hands."

"She really was amazing," Lucy enthuses, smiling up at Dad.

He puts his arm around her.

There's a loud groan from behind us. Callahan has come round and has rolled on to his back. Propping himself up on his elbows, he blinks to focus on the group of silhouettes surrounding him.

His eyes scan across the animals and widen in fear. The crocodile snaps his jaws once.

Callahan lets out a high-pitched squeal and rolls back on to his front to try to crawl away, but Nan has stealthily placed her shoe on his lab coat so that he wriggles around on the floor to no avail.

"I think it would be best if you stop squirming," she tells him haughtily. "This happens to be one of my favourite pans, and I would hate to have to use it against your head again and risk denting it."

He instantly lies still.

"Very good," she says with a nod of approval. "You can stay where you are until the police come to get you. Attacking children, kidnapping people, actioning an evil plan to capture these beautiful animals" – she tuts loudly – "you have a lot of explaining to do."

Callahan whimpers.

"Now, Luna, may I suggest that these animals go back to their other forms before the police storm the place?" Nan continues calmly. "I believe Athena wanted this project to remain secret for a reason – the fewer people who know what these creatures can do, the better."

"You're right." I nod. "I'm not really sure how to do that, but…"

There's a searing flash of blue light and when it's gone, the animals are back to normal. I look at them all in amazement.

"How do they know?" I ask, chuckling as the ferret comes scampering over and crawls up to rest on my cradled forearm.

"They're connected to you, remember?" Callahan mutters bitterly.

Nan clears her throat. "Excuse me, did I say *you* could talk?"

He winces and falls silent again. Nan turns to me with a warm smile and places a hand on my shoulder as I get to my feet.

"They're connected to you," she repeats in a wise and authoritative manner. "I always said you were a special girl, didn't I? Knew it all along."

"Thank you so much for saving us," Lucy says, addressing me, Kieron and Nan. "You three are quite the rescue team."

I share a smile with Kieron and then shrug. "We're family."

"Quite a strange family, but a family nonetheless!" Kieron laughs as the sparrow flits through the air to land on my head, the gecko crawls on to my shoe and the tabby cat starts hissing at Silver as he gives her a warning growl in return.

"I do have one last question before the police arrive," Dad announces. He takes a dramatic pause and then poses it: "Where exactly are all these animals going to live?"

The room falls into silence.

We all turn to look at Nan expectantly, the animals included.

She lifts her eyes to the ceiling.

"Oh, for goodness' sake," she groans, letting out a sigh as she caves to our hopeful expressions. "Right, we're going to need to set some ground rules."

# CHAPTER EIGHTEEN

"Drop that cabbage at once, you NAUGHTY FERRET!"

I grimace at Nan's cry in the kitchen, rushing in from the garden to check what's going on. Nan is frantically shooing Blizzard, the ferret, away from her cooking, grumbling about how cheeky he is being today as he dances around the kitchen counters, evading her.

"There you are, Luna," Nan huffs,

shaking a wooden spoon at me. "Do you know how difficult it is to cater for a large group of people?"

I glance over my shoulder at our extended family milling around the garden, chatting away in the sunshine to all of Nan's neighbours who she invited to join us Sunday for lunch.

"Um, I'm guessing it's quite difficult," I reply as Silver plods over to sit at my feet.

"You would be right. Now, tell me this, do you think that task is made any easier by a FERRET tucking into my dishes when he doesn't think I'm looking?"

I shake my head.

"Please remove your ferret from my kitchen," she instructs, pointing her finger at the door.

"Blizzard, come on," I say, ushering him over to me.

Making a hissing noise that sounds a little like he's sniggering, Blizzard bolts across the kitchen and I bend down to lift him up into my arms.

"You tell that ferret that if he doesn't start behaving, he's going to be packing his little ferret bags any day now, and he'll have to find a new home elsewhere," Nan mutters, opening the fridge and rummaging about inside. "This morning he swiped my toast right off my plate! And that was after he dunked his entire head into the jam. His ENTIRE HEAD, Luna. I had to throw that jar out, and I'd only just bought it from Nigel in my choir group. When he's not busy travelling the world bungee jumping, he makes jam to sell at the farmer's market. He doesn't make it often, Luna, and now that whole jar has gone to waste."

"Sorry about that, Nan, I'll have a word with Blizzard," I assure her as he blinks up at me innocently, and I give him a tickle under the chin.

"Lot of good that will do," she huffs. "That mischievous ferret doesn't respect authority. Did I tell you what happened yesterday when I was running my bubble bath? I poured in all those lovely new salts that Lucy got me, got it to the perfect temperature, went into my room to find my book, returned to the bath, and guess who I found in there, splashing about, treating the place like a water park?"

338

I have already heard this story several times since the incident yesterday, but I play along, deciding it's best to give her the satisfaction of having a good rant.

"Naughty Blizzard," I answer.

"Naughty Blizzard *indeed*," she emphasizes, shaking a whisk in Blizzard's direction as he lets out a yawn, unbothered by her tone. "That's the second time he's commandeered my bath, Luna, turning on the cold-water tap and ruining it completely. It's meant to be a relaxing atmosphere. Let me tell you, a ferret gliding back and forth under the water, leaping around like some kind of hyperactive miniature seal does not create the soothing ambiance I'm after."

"Ferrets do tend to like water," I remind her apologetically, before glancing around me to check that no one else is listening as I quietly add, "not to mention polar bears are partial to it too."

"I don't care if that creature can turn into a *dolphin*," Nan says indignantly, shaking some thyme into a pot. "I do NOT share my baths, is that clear?"

I nod vigorously. "Crystal."

"Good. Now can you please bring the salads out on to the table?"

Lifting Blizzard up on to my shoulder where he likes to curl himself around my neck, I hurry to grab the two large salad bowls from where they're sitting on the counter and carry them into the garden, setting them carefully down on the table that's already heaving with Nan's amazing dishes. Just as I place them down, I notice one of the salad leaves moves, and a small green head pops up from underneath.

"Chomp, get out of the salad!" I hiss. "Quick, before Nan sees!"

My gecko crawls from the bowl on to my hand, looking very pleased with himself.

"Honestly, you lot need to start behaving. If we're not careful, Nan is going to throw all of us out."

Silver nudges me with his nose and I smile down at him, reaching to stroke his head.

"Of course you're perfectly behaved already, Silver," I assure him. "You're very…"

I trail off because Stripes has jumped up on to the

table and started teasing Silver by swishing her tail back and forth right in front of his snout. He lets out a warning growl, his eyes flashing playfully at her, and I know exactly what's coming.

Despite being dog and cat, Silver and Stripes are the best of friends, although Stripes definitely has the upper hand – she prefers Silver's big dog bed to the lovely new one Dad bought for her, so she sleeps there while poor Silver is left to curl up in her bed that's half his size. She also enjoys teasing Silver on a daily basis, flicking her tail like a pendulum in front of his face until he's riled up enough to chase her around the garden. She happily jumps on to the fence where he can't reach her. We already had an instance yesterday where Silver lost control during this game just as I grabbed him to try to calm him down, and suddenly there was a wolf chasing a tabby cat through Nan's petunias. A moment later when I tried to catch Stripes, a tiger was darting around the geraniums too.

Poor Mr Piffle who lives next door happened

to be looking out of his window at the time and thought the bad avocado he'd eaten for breakfast was making him hallucinate.

All of us got a long lecture from Nan after that.

"Silver," I warn through gritted teeth as the fur on his back stands on end in anticipation of a chase, "don't you dare. Stripes, today is not a good day for this game, got it? Please wait until everyone has left and—"

I don't get to finish. There's a huge commotion as Silver lunges at Stripes's tail, missing it by an inch as she takes off, leaping over Nan's dishes along the table and jumping up on to the side of the fence as Silver races along beside her, barking his head off. I bury my head in my hands, praying that Nan is too distracted in the kitchen to take much notice. Luckily, the guests find the disturbance amusing, laughing at the two of them as they race around the garden, before they return to their pleasant conversations.

I hear a small flutter of wings by my ear as Talon comes to land on my shoulder.

"What *are* we going to do with them?" I ask her, using the knuckle of my forefinger to stroke her chest.

She shakes her tail feathers in response, communicating that she doesn't have time for their nonsense and I chuckle, acknowledging her lofty nature.

Since the animals moved in to Nan's, it's been absolute chaos in the very best way. I've loved getting to know each of their personalities: Stripes the cat is clever and elegant; Chomp the gecko is curious and fun; Blizzard the ferret is a whirlwind of activity and is always getting in trouble; Talon the sparrow is sophisticated and superior; and we already know that Silver is amazingly loyal and loving.

The first day living alongside this new team was a bit of a trial – I thought Nan might implode with the amount of mess that Blizzard managed to leave in his wake, but it didn't take long for everyone to settle down nicely into a routine and, as much as she likes to complain about all of them, I've also never seen her laugh so often either. She likes to talk to all of them as she bustles around and, although I know

343

she doesn't have a favourite, I think she particularly enjoys it when Talon graces her with her company. Talon will swoop in and perch on the drying rack next to the sink while Nan reels off all her complaints.

"Look at you," Aunty Gracie says to me as she wanders over to the food table, flanked by Aunty Shirley and Uncle Desmond. She nods to the bird on my shoulder. "It's extraordinary. You have the spirit of your mum."

Uncle Desmond nods, smiling fondly. "When Athena was your age, she was always outside, rescuing some kind of animal in distress. Once she came home with a pig, brought it right into the house. You should have seen Nan's face!"

"Oh yes, I remember that!" Aunty Gracie laughs. "In the holidays, she'd beg Nan to go swimming in the sea every day, even in the rain, so she could try to spot a manatee."

"I've been reading about the manatee," I tell them enthusiastically. "Beautiful sea creatures that you can find off the coast of Jamaica, but they're endangered, right?"

"That's right." Aunty Gracie nods, beaming at me. "You know, Luna, there's something different about you these days. I can't quite put my finger on it."

"You're right, Gracie, something has changed," agrees Uncle Desmond. "It could be a growth spurt."

"No, she hasn't grown again," remarks Aunty Shirley with a knowing smile. "She's hunching less."

"Yes, that's it." Uncle Desmond nods. "You're standing taller!"

"Am I?" I say in surprise. "I didn't notice that I was doing that."

"Happiness shows itself in all manner of ways," says Aunty Shirley wisely. She pauses, frowning as she glances down into the salad bowl. "I could have sworn I just saw a gecko on that salad spoon!"

"Luna, tell us all about the new school you're starting on Tuesday," requests Uncle Desmond. "Are you nervous? Or are you excited?"

"Yes, what are you most looking forward to?" Aunty Gracie asks. "Have you got all your supplies yet? I hope your father hasn't left them to the last minute!"

"Nan would never let that happen," Aunty Shirley points out. "What are your favourite subjects at school, Luna? Science, like your mum? That's what you'll need to do well in if you want to go into the veterinary profession, which it seems like you should!"

"She's only twelve," reasons Uncle Desmond. "Bit too early to think about her career! Tell me, Luna, what sports do you enjoy?"

"And do you play any musical instruments?"

"I think you should try out for drama club! A nice, tall girl like you would probably get the lead role with such a great stage presence."

"And what about art? Have you tried any sketching? I was always good at sketching; it runs in the family. Would you like me to get you some pencils for your next birthday?"

Attempting to process their questions, I burst out laughing, placing a hand on Silver's head as he plods over to sit next to me, resting his head against my leg after an exhausting chase around the garden with Stripes. A few weeks ago, this kind of attention from my loud, fabulous family would have been enough to make me break out in a sweat, make up some kind of excuse and run away to lock myself in my bedroom. But with my animals at my side, and after everything that's happened this summer, I've discovered a new confidence. I'll never be someone who's comfortable in the spotlight, but I definitely feel somehow more at ease with myself.

I've proven to myself that I don't have to be invisible.

"You've found your home at last, haven't you, Luna?" Nan remarked yesterday, smiling to herself after I came in from running around the garden with the animals, my cheeks flushed with laughter.

And I think she's right. I don't feel lost any more.

After trying to answer as many of the questions flying at me from my aunts and uncle as possible – I'm both nervous and excited about school, but mostly pleased that I'm going to the same one as Kieron; I enjoy science and definitely want to one day work with animals; I like some sports; I'm not very good at drama, art or any musical instrument, but maybe I'll give them a try anyway – I catch Lucy's eye across the garden and excuse myself when she gestures for me to join her.

"I've just been chatting to Tina, your nan's neighbour who lives two doors down," Lucy informs me, reaching out to pet Blizzard, who is still wrapped around my neck. "She was asking me whether I knew if hamsters could be toilet-trained. I think her daughter's hamster is mistaking the sofa cushions for its private bathroom."

"I overheard Nan telling Tina earlier that if she thinks a hamster is hard work, she should try practising salsa dancing with an unruly ferret jumping on her shoes."

"That does sound tricky!" Lucy laughs, shaking her head. "Before I forget, I wanted to talk to you about something, but feel free to tell me that you're not interested."

"What is it?"

"A friend of mine runs an animal sanctuary in Jamaica and I've been discussing it with your dad and, well, I thought that maybe it might be fun for the four of us to go on holiday to Jamaica in your next school holidays, and maybe help out a bit there, learning about all those different animals he looks after," she blurts out hurriedly, trying to gauge my reaction as she speaks. "But I completely understand if you'd rather not; you might not want to go on holiday all together quite yet, so you can think about it and let your dad know how you feel and we can—"

"Lucy," I interrupt, "that sounds wonderful!"

Her expression brightens as she breathes a sigh of relief. "Really? It does?"

"Yeah, I'd love to."

Silver lets out a grumpy bark from where he's sitting at my feet, and I roll my eyes.

"Yes, Silver, you would of course be coming too," I assure him, before looking up at Lucy apologetically. "We'd have to find a way of travelling with the animals."

"I'm sure we can sort something. That's great!" She beams. "Thanks, Luna." She glances over my shoulder. "Ah … I think your dad wants to talk to you. He looks a little … stressed."

I turn round to see Dad pulling a face by the food, and he stealthily jabs his finger to where Stripes is sitting on the table, licking the butter. I rush over and swipe the butter dish out from under her nose.

"Stripes, no!" I scold, while she licks her whiskers contentedly.

"Don't worry, Nan didn't see," Dad assures me. "Besides, I think she has a soft spot for Stripes. I caught her grooming her the other day with a little cat comb she'd bought for her."

"I thought Nan had a soft spot for Talon. They

like to have a morning gossip over a cup of tea," I point out.

"Lucy thought Nan's favourite was Chomp. She found little bowls of chopped apricots in the fridge, and when Lucy asked if she could have some, Nan said no because she'd prepared those specially for Chomp. He's very fond of apricot, she said."

"That's funny, because Kieron insisted that Blizzard was the one who'd won over Nan as he makes her laugh so much."

Silver nudges me with his nose.

"Good point, Silver," I continue, giving his ears a scratch. "Nan adores you, and you were here first."

"I think they're *all* her favourites," Dad concludes. "Who would have thought it?"

"Mum would be happy to see Nan with all these animals, I reckon," I say quietly, placing a hand over my pendant and gripping it within my fingers.

Dad nods and, throwing his arm around my shoulders, leads me to the side of the garden to a couple of chairs that Nan has put out, away from the crowd for a moment. He sits down in one and gestures for me to sit in the other facing him.

"I've been meaning to tell you, Luna," he begins, lowering his voice, "when your mum got sick, whatever happened she was adamant that her necklace would end up with you and only you. She didn't waver on that – it couldn't go to her mum or to her sisters or any of her nieces. I always thought it was simply because she wanted her jewellery to be worn by her daughter, but now I think it was much more than that." His eyes glisten as he takes a deep breath. "I believe that your mother knew there was magic in you. That's why it had to be you who wore the necklace."

Silver rests his head in my lap.

"Thanks, Dad," I say softly, smiling up at him.

He reaches over to squeeze my hand. "I'm very proud of you, Luna. Not just because of the magic, but because you've been brilliant about the move to London and welcoming Lucy and Kieron – it's meant a lot. All that matters to me is that you're happy."

"I am, Dad," I say in all sincerity. "And you were right all along. It really has been an exciting new adventure."

"Yes." He hesitates. "But I think we may have had enough adventure for now, don't you?"

We laugh together before Dad starts looking about the garden in confusion. "Where's Kieron? I haven't seen him in a while."

"He's writing."

Dad raises his eyebrows. "Tell him if he's not careful, he's going to miss out on all the food. Especially when Stripes is hanging about," he adds with a wink. "I'll add butter to the shopping list tomorrow. Nan never needs to know."

"Agreed. I'll go find Kieron now."

Heading in from the garden party, I leave Silver to help Nan decide on an appropriate summery playlist to blast out through the speakers and make my way through to the sitting room where Kieron is sitting on the sofa, typing furiously at his laptop. He's so engrossed in his writing, he doesn't notice me come in at first.

"You almost done?" I ask, standing in front of him. "You're going to miss out on all the food."

"Hang on just one more minute," he requests, his forehead creased in fierce concentration.

Sitting down next to him, I wait patiently as he finishes up the paragraph and saves the document before closing it.

"How's the story going?" I ask.

"I think it's good, but it's hard to tell." He shrugs, sliding his glasses up his nose.

Even though we've decided to keep the animals and their magical abilities a secret from the world, Kieron wanted to keep an accurate record of everything that happened this summer, so he's written a journal-style story about our adventures, starting right from the beginning when Dad and I moved to London. He hasn't let me take a peek at it yet, and I keep pestering him to finish so I can finally read it. Kieron is a perfectionist, and he keeps telling me that he's only on the first draft so it will be a while until I get to read the final version. I already know it will be brilliant, though.

"I need to show you something," Kieron says, opening his emails.

"Are you finally going to let me read something you've written?"

"Nope," he says sternly to my disappointment, "but I thought you should see this. I just received it from the same mystery person who sent me the unpublished article about Magnitude."

He opens an email and then swivels the laptop screen towards me so I can read it:

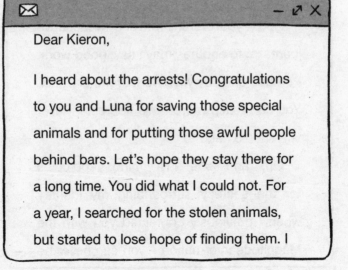

Dear Kieron,

I heard about the arrests! Congratulations to you and Luna for saving those special animals and for putting those awful people behind bars. Let's hope they stay there for a long time. You did what I could not. For a year, I searched for the stolen animals, but started to lose hope of finding them. I couldn't be happier they are safe again!

I wonder if you could write back to let me know the animals have a home? I looked after them for a time, but if they are happy where they are, then I will gladly take this opportunity to leave them be, and travel and write as I used to. It's been a while since I put pen to paper.

If you would be so kind as to send Luna my best wishes – I was a friend of her mother's. From what I can tell, she seems so like her.

And to you, Kieron, from one investigative journalist to another, may I say: good work. Perhaps one day we'll work together again. You can reach me on this address, if ever you should need to.

Oh, and one last thing, apologies for the secrecy surrounding my identity when I previously contacted you with the Magnitude information – you can never be

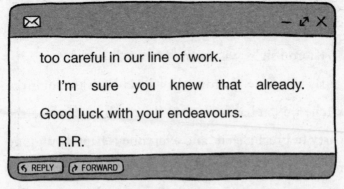

too careful in our line of work.

I'm sure you knew that already.

Good luck with your endeavours.

R.R.

REPLY   FORWARD

After reading the email, I look up at Kieron in confusion. "R.R.?"

"Rex Robinson." Kieron grins. "Callahan mentioned him in the lab. He was the journalist that your mum leaked the story to, the one who was looking after the animals until he broke his foot. I've looked into him, and he has written some incredible stories throughout his career. There are theories that he's done loads more articles too under different names. He's held huge corporations to account, brought global awareness to important issues, bravely questioned powerful leaders … he's an *inspiration*."

"So, this is the guy who helped my mum rescue the animals? She must have really trusted him." I smile at the screen, glancing over the email again. "I hope one day we get to meet him."

Kieron sighs wistfully. "Me too."

By the time Kieron and I head back through the kitchen, Nan has turned up the music and joined the party to great cheers, and everyone is happily digging into the delicious food. We notice that Silver appears to have been snuck a plate of food in the kitchen with a little bit of everything on there for him. He licks his chops as he finishes up.

"Did Nan set aside a special plate of food for you, Silver?" I ask curiously.

He burps in reply. Kieron and I confidently agree that there's no doubt about it: Nan has officially been won over.

We hold back on joining everyone for a moment, the two of us standing by the kitchen door with Silver, looking out into the sunny garden where family and friends are chatting away over good food. Dad and Lucy share a kiss when they think no one's looking. Nan is showing off her dance moves to Tina from two doors down. Stripes is curled up in the lap of one of my cousins. Blizzard has leapt down from around my neck and wound his way through the crowd to pounce on Nan's unsuspecting dancing feet. Talon is perched on the edge of the birdbath, pompously surveying the guests. Chomp is a little trickier to see, but I eventually spot him on the tablecloth, eyeing up the fruit salad Nan's put out for pudding.

"By the way, I've decided on a title for my story," Kieron informs me, folding his arms and leaning against the door frame.

"Oh yeah? What is it?" I ask.

"*Adventures of an Animal Wizard*," he announces. "What do you think?"

Before I can answer, Silver throws his head back and lets out a resounding howl.

"I think that means Silver approves," I declare. "It's perfect, Kieron. I love it."

Sharing a grin, we head out to join our family in the sunshine, with my dog, as ever, right by my side.

# EPILOGUE

Callahan hasn't had one visitor in prison.

No one has come to see him since his arrest. He supposes he shouldn't be surprised. It's not like he has any friends or family that he still speaks to. His obsession with Magnitude had taken over his life and everything else fell away. The only people he can call close to being friends are Dean and Chad, and they hardly count. For a start, he'd hired them, so they didn't hang around him by choice. And what's more, Callahan *detests* both of them. Their bickering, their stupidity, their oafishness — he can't bear that he's been reduced to keeping such company.

He's already heard that Dean has been stupid enough to tell the police the full story. Apparently, the moment they left that warehouse and were slapped straight into cuffs by the police waiting outside, Dean blabbed about everything. What a *fool*. They didn't believe him for a moment! Word is that when Dean comes to trial, his sentence could be even longer due to an extra charge of wasting police time and obscuring an investigation by telling such absurd porkies about his run-in with a real-life polar bear.

So, there is at least one positive about being holed up in a prison cell. At least Callahan doesn't have to put up with Dean and Chad.

Lying on the rock-hard mattress and staring up at the dark ceiling of his cell, he sighs, haunted by the idea that he was *so close* to getting everything he wanted. He was back in his laboratory, he had the animals, AND he had the last remnants of the magical source. How could it have gone so wrong?

The Wolf girl. This is all her fault. He is cursed by that family.

A loud knocking jolts Callahan from his thoughts.

"You've got a visitor," the guard tells him through the door.

Callahan sits up in surprise as the heavily bolted door is unlocked and pushed open with an eerie creaking sound. The silhouette of a large, suited figure forms in his doorway.

Callahan gasps, scrambling to his feet and standing to attention.

"Good evening, Callahan," the visitor says in a low growl.

"Y-you're here. I didn't think that—"

"The plan failed then," the man interrupts impatiently.

Callahan's eyes drop to the floor. "Y-yes, sir. We were so close, but the plan was foiled by—"

"I know exactly who it is that got in the way. It would seem that she has the same talents and abilities as her mother."

"Yes," Callahan confirms bitterly. "So it would appear."

The man glances around the prison cell. "It's very dreary in here. I think you've spent enough time wallowing about in prison. Don't you?"

Callahan looks up hopefully. "You can get me out?"

"I can do whatever I want. Besides, I need you for the new plan."

"There's a new plan?"

"Did you really think I would let a little girl get away with *my* magic and *my* animals? A long time ago, I told you that in the end I wouldn't let anyone get in my way."

Callahan looks up at him in awe.

"You may have failed me once again, Callahan," his visitor continues, "but I trust that you will not fail me this time. Especially as I've gone to so much trouble to get you an early release from prison."

"Yes, sir. I mean, no, sir. I mean, I will not fail you again, sir," Callahan assures him.

"Come along then. We have work to do." A sinister smile creeps across the man's lips as he turns to leave. "After all, how much trouble can one little girl be?"

# ACKNOWLEDGEMENTS

I'm super excited to be back with a brand new book! I have always felt a deep connection and love for animals, I grew up with them and I've been fortunate enough to work alongside some of the best animal charities in the world that do incredible work to protect them. I believe that all animals are special in their own unique way, it's a privilege to be around them and you can learn so much from them! It was only a matter of time before I featured them as the stars in one of my books! A big thank you to my mum who taught me how to love and respect them and the wonderful Katie Hobbs who I've shared many animal adventures with.

Other animal loving humans that I'm so lucky to work with are Lauren Fortune, Sarah Dutton, Aimee Stewart, Beth Mincher, Rachel Phillipps, Hannah Griffiths, Lauren Gardner, Justine Smith and Paul Moreton. Thank you for all of your efforts, hard work and passion! Thank you to Deise Lino for the gorgeous art and thank you to the wonderful Katy Birchall for her creative genius once again! Thank you to my family for their brilliant ideas and input and a big thank you to all of the readers who continue to support me.

I have the BEST team who make every part of this process such a joy! I hope you enjoy this book as much as we loved creating it!

Be kind to animals and each other!

Love always

Alesha X

Photo by Aimee Stewart

Katy Birchall is the author of the side-splittingly funny *How Not To Be a Vampire Slayer* and *A Vampire Slayer's Survival Guide*, the *Morgan Charmley: Teen Witch* books, *The It Girl* series and the *Hotel Royale* series, *Secrets of a Teenage Heiress* and *Dramas of a Teenage Heiress*, and the *Find the Girl* YA series with YouTube stars Lucy and Lydia Connell. Katy was proud to be the author of a retelling of Jane Austen's *Emma* for the Awesomely Austen series, a collection of Austen's novels retold for younger readers, and the spin-off novel for the hit Netflix TV show, *Sex Education*. Katy also works as a freelance journalist and has written a non-fiction book, *How to be a Princess: Real-Life Fairy Tales for Modern Heroines*.

She has written two novels for adults, *The Secret Bridesmaid* and *The Wedding Season*.

Katy lives in London with her husband Ben, and her rescue dog Bono.

Don't miss Alesha's
high-voltage, laugh-out-loud,
mega-bestselling
LIGHTNING GIRL series!

Photo by John Wright

Turn over for a sneak peek

No one ever warned me that when you get angry, bright sparks might explode from your fingertips.

But that's exactly what happened. One minute I was watching some school bullies round on my little sister in the playground, and the next minute my hands went all hot and tingly and suddenly these beams of light came flying out from my palms, like a lightning storm.

I think I scared myself more than anyone

else. No one actually saw where the sparks came from, just a flash of blinding light behind them, and then when they turned around, there I was staring wide-eyed at my hands and madly wiggling my fingers.

One of the girls snorted as she watched me bring my hand right up to my face, so it was almost touching the end of my nose, and examine my little finger closely.

"Isn't that your older sister, Clara?" she sneered. "What on earth is she *doing*?"

"She's as odd as you are!" sniggered another one, as they all looked me up and down. I gulped.

Getting them to pick on me instead of Clara wasn't *technically* my original plan. I figured I would just tell them to leave her alone, rather than distract them by becoming a human firework. Still, they weren't interested in Clara any more and it seemed that they weren't all that curious about a random and inexplicable burst of light in the middle of the playground either.

So that was something.

"What do you want, Aurora?" a tall boy said to me, raising his eyebrows.

"U-um. . ." I stammered, my hands still held up in front of my face. "I was just, uh, looking at my . . . scar."

I held out my left hand, so they could see the swirled scar across my palm.

"I was born with it. Weird, isn't it? Scars appear when the skin tissue heals over a wound to protect and strengthen it. Interesting. Right?"

Imagine swapping lives with your
favourite pop star...

STAR
SWITCH

ALESHA
DIXON

FROM
THE AUTHOR OF
BESTSELLING SERIES
LIGHTNING GIRL

Imagine if your mum was the most powerful woman in the country...

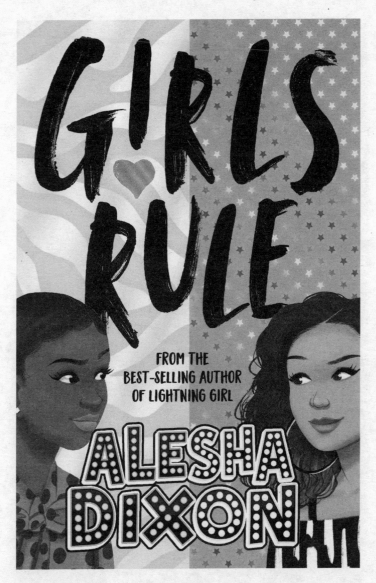

GIRLS RULE

FROM THE
BEST-SELLING AUTHOR
OF LIGHTNING GIRL

ALESHA DIXON